THE HIDDEN YEARS

— A NOVEL —

W.D. Spruill

NEWMAN SPRINGS PUBLISHING
320 Broad Street
Red Bank, NJ 07701

First originally published by Newman Springs Publishing 2021

ISBN 978-1-63881-710-9 (Paperback)
ISBN 978-1-63881-711-6 (Digital)

Printed in the United States of America

TO MY WIFE, PATRICIA, I dedicate this book and sincerely hope that the next fifty years of our marriage will be as good as the first fifty years, barring the eight years I was incarcerated. God allowed me to be incarcerated so I could be still and know that he is God (Psalm 46:10).

CONTENTS

PREFACE

O THE READERS WHO chose to read this work of fiction, I thank you for your patience and open-mindedness.

In the course of the apostles writing the Synoptic Gospels, many questions were raised but not answered. This literary work in no means infringes on the writing of the apostles and their effort to detail the life of Christ Jesus.

What I have tried to do is answer some age-old questions that have gone unanswered since the scriptures were put together at the Council of Trent. I tried to write, answering the questions in an informative way and also fun to read.

I did take some liberties with locations and timelines. In doing so, I tried to set the stage in many instances for the parables that Christ used in his teachings; the characters that Christ called to his ministry; the bond between him and John the Baptist and his friends Mary, Martha, and Lazarus; and how Judas Iscariot targeted Christ's ministry to become a hanger-on.

Some events and timelines are taken out of the Infancy Gospel attributed to Apostle Thomas.

Other events, such as why John the Baptist; his mother, Elizabeth; and his father, Zechariah, escaped the decree of Herod the Great to slaughter all the infants two years of age or younger in and around Bethlehem and Judea was not explained in the Bible.

Both Jesus and John the Baptist were within six months of age.

This question was not answered in the books of Matthew, Mark, Luke, and John.

In Cana, at the wedding, did Jesus tell his mother that his "time had not come" and then turn and change the water to wine?

In no way is this work authenticated by Bible scholars but is used strictly as a reference point in my narrative of Christ's early life that is not covered in the Scriptures.

I have tried not to add or take anything away from the Scriptures as written by the apostles (Revelation 22:18).

To my readers, I thank you and ask you to read this work with an open mind and heart and enjoy it as much as I have enjoyed writing and trying in my own humble way to answer some questions that have plagued me since I started reading the Bible.

PART 1

AD 6

Passover Week, Jerusalem

CHAPTER 1

THE BEGINNING

"MOTHER, DID YOU NOT know that I must be about my Father's business?"

Mary and Joseph stood in the synagogue's courtyard looking at their twelve-year-old son, who was surrounded by the teachers and priests of the temple.

Mary did not know how to answer her son other than to reprimand him for straying from the crowd that had come to the Passover Festival.

As any frightened and worried mother would be, she was only thinking about her earthly son and not the divine character of Jesus that both she and Joseph had been revealed.

It is funny how the mundane things of everyday living can veil our eyes to the glory of God and get us so wrapped up in our own worries we forget about the real important things in our lives.

Later, as the caravan journeyed back toward Nazareth, Mary and Joseph had ample time to discuss the festival and all that had happened while they were in Jerusalem.

"Joseph," Mary asked, "why did Jesus get so involved with the temple teachers and priests that he would not be aware that we would be looking for him when he was not with the caravan?"

All Joseph could do was look at his wife and conclude and think back on that night that the angel appeared to him and told him to "not be afraid, for Mary carried the child of the Holy Spirit," and to marry her.

Somehow Joseph understood. Just as El Shaddai was the silent guiding hand of mankind, Joseph was to be the silent guiding hand of Jesus, the Messiah.

Mary looked at her husband and inquired again what she meant, as if Joseph had not heard her question.

Joseph stumbled on some rough ground as they walked along, and looked at his wife and said, "It is ordained, and we must be vigilant to his every need" (Matthew 1:20–21).

The caravan had stopped for the night as they were still a ways from Nazareth, and all were tired and hungry.

As Mary got the camp set up for the evening meal, Joseph set up the tents while Jesus was playing with the other boys in the caravan.

As most kids do, there was shouting and pushing, and they were engaged in roughhouse play. Jesus, being a typical kid of a carpenter, engaged in this play also.

As Mary readied the evening meal, she realized she had no water in the water jugs for the meal.

She called for Jesus but could not get his attention, so she took a jug and hurried off to the water wagon to fill the jug with her needs.

As Mary hurried along between the tents and camps of the other travelers, she passed the camp of her friend Rebecca and her family.

She heard Rebecca's son Abraham say, "But, Mother, it is true, I did see it! Benjamin pushed Jesus, and he started to fall, but he did not hit the ground. It is true. I did see it! It was as if something held him up from falling to the ground. It was as if something, something held him up from the ground. I did see it. Mother, I do not lie. Please believe me.

"Just like the other day, when we were playing around a mud puddle after the rain on the Sabbath, Jesus wanted some animals to play with, so he made some animals and birds out of mud. Then he clapped his hands, and they started walking around and the birds flew away" (Infancy Gospel 15:1).

"Aw, no one believes me anyway. Mother, it is the truth."

Mary stopped for a short time pondering these things, but she carried on with her mission.

She would have to discuss these things with Joseph after the evening meal and the children had gone to bed.

CHAPTER 2

THE BOND

"**J**OHN, COME HERE AND get washed up for the evening meal."

As Elizabeth readied the evening meal, she wondered to herself, *Why in the name of Yahweh does John have to play with the bugs and creatures in the dirt?*

She understood his fascination with the living creatures, but when he told her that he had eaten berries and dead locusts, she almost lost her appetite that day.

He had told her that a "voice" told him that locusts would be what he would eat in the desert, along with honey and water from the Jordan River.

She had just waved it off as a child's phase and a fantasy he was going through.

"I am here, Mother."

Elizabeth looked up from the pot she was stirring. And there stood John, all thirteen years of him, covered with dirt and, heaven's name, a coat of animal skin.

"John! Where in the world did you get that coat?"

John looked at her as only a child could and said it was a gift from their "neighbor."

"He told me it would keep me warm when I will be in the desert," answered John.

"John, you go take that coat off right now. Wash up for supper and evening prayers before your father comes home from the synagogue."

John shuffled off to his room and took the coat off, and even though it was a little big for him, the "man" said it would fit him and he would grow into it.

John folded the coat and laid it under his pillow so it would be close to him.

After Zechariah returned from the local synagogue, evening prayers were said, with John participating in them with vigor.

John especially enjoyed the scrolls of Isaiah and all the scriptures concerning the coming of the Messiah and the forerunner paving the way for the Anointed One.

But there were many scrolls also that bothered John, and when he inquired with his father, Zechariah could not offer an answer to them, especially in Jeremiah where Yahweh was telling Jeremiah there would come a time when Yahweh would give the people of Israel a new covenant not based on the law he had handed down at Mt. Sinai to their ancestors but they would be written on the people's minds and hearts—a new covenant so each man would know God's commandments and not have to teach them to each other (Jeremiah 31).

These and many other scriptures puzzled John and made him think about them when he was alone.

As prayers ended, they sat down to eat the evening meal and to give thanks to Yahweh for all he had given them. As Zechariah began to break the bread and pass it to John, Elizabeth sensed something in John that was not normal.

Elizabeth asked John, "Are you all right tonight, my son?"

John looked down at his meal of lamb and vegetables, wanting to confide in his mother, but under the circumstances, John first had to talk to his father, Zechariah.

John sat at the table wanting to tell his parents he had been thinking about his cousin and it had been a while since they had seen each other. Yes, John had seen both Jesus, Mary, Joseph, and the other children; but they were not the same age as Jesus and him.

Just then, Zechariah spoke to Elizabeth and John, "In a few days, I must travel to Jerusalem to the temple and fulfill my obligation as temple priest for the allotted time.

"Elizabeth, this would be a wonderful time, for Mary and Jesus could come and spend some time with you and John.

"On the morrow, send word to Mary in Nazareth and see if Joseph can spare Jesus for a while and if they could come and stay with you and John while I am away."

At this, John's heart leapt in his small chest, and he could hardly sit still.

"Oh, Mother, would you?" John said aloud. He was unaware that he had said it aloud but thought he had only thought it.

As John sat there thinking to himself, Elizabeth said, "As you wish, my husband, I will see to it tomorrow."

CHAPTER 3

THE INVITATION

TWO SABBATHS HAD PASSED since Elizabeth had sent the scroll to Mary in Nazareth, and she was beginning to wonder if Mary had received the communiqué.

She tried to put it out of her mind and prayed that Yahweh, Jireh, would provide the answer she prayed for.

Just as she was setting the noon meal on the table, there was an excited voice from out front of the house, which could only be John's.

"Mother! Mother! Come quickly. There is a messenger here looking for the wife of Zechariah the temple priest."

Elizabeth dropped her towel, wiped her hands on her apron, and hurried out the door to see the young man standing in the gateway of the yard.

"Are you the wife of Zechariah the temple priest?" he inquired.

Elizabeth looked puzzled with the formality of the young man but did not question his sincerity with the message. "Yes, I am Elizabeth."

The young man, slim in stature and fair of skin and hair, smiled at her and then John. "I have a scroll from Mary, mother of Jesus in Nazareth."

This line of dialogue puzzled Elizabeth as it was not normal to denote the child of a mother as the reason for something.

As Elizabeth took the scroll from the young messenger, John was standing next to her in the yard, trying to see as best he could the writing on the scroll. When Elizabeth unrolled the scroll, she glanced up, and the messenger was gone in front of her. She looked all around to see if he was there, but he had vanished into thin air, it seemed to her.

Dear cousin Elizabeth, Zechariah, and John,

It was extremely good to hear from you in your scroll and offer Jesus and I to come and spend some time with you and John while Zechariah is away in Jerusalem.

I discussed the visit with Joseph, and since this time of the year his work is slow, and with what work he has, James, his son, and the other children to help around the shop and home, he thought it would be a good idea for John and Jesus to spend some time together.

We pray Yahweh will bless our journey and see us safely to your home.

Blessed be to you and John as well as Zechariah.

Until we meet,
Your cousin Mary

So Elizabeth thought, *Yahweh, bless this trip, and his grace and mercy will follow them as the journey unfolds. Praise Yahweh for his blessings to behold.*

CHAPTER 4

THE JOURNEY

"**H**URRY UP, JESUS," CRIED Mary. "We need to get the rest of the gifts and supplies on the cart and be off to meet the caravan."

Jesus was wondering if he should take an extra pair of sandals with him in case he might need them. "Mother, should I take an extra pair of sandals with me?"

Mary thought to herself and wondered if this child really was the chosen Messiah as the heavenly host had proclaimed. She smiled to herself and said, *Of course, he is. He is just a child finding his way in the world.*

"Yes!" exclaimed Mary. "It is better to be safe than to need something and not have it. Be prepared, son" (Matthew 25:1–12).

Jesus grabbed his other pair of sandals, tucked them under his arm, and ran out of the door, saying goodbye to James and the other children.

"Father," Jesus said as he kissed his father on the cheek, "I'll study the scrolls as often as I can."

Joseph smiled at himself and then looked at Mary, for Joseph knew that Jesus would do as he said he would. For Joseph knew Yahweh could not and would not lie.

*****

Jesus guided the donkey and cart with all the gifts and supplies they would need on the journey on the rutted road where years and years of travelers had trod, from the days of King Solomon and his father, the great king David.

Jesus's mind wandered to the time that this was no more than a goat path, when God sent his angel to stand in the way of Balaam's she-donkey as he was riding to meet the servants of Balak with the servants of Moa'als (Numbers 22:22).

Jesus laughed under his breath at the surprise of Balaam when Balaam cursed the donkey for crushing his leg against the stone wall on either side of the path.

How surprised was Balaam when the angel of the Lord opened Balaam's eyes so he could see the angel in the path ahead of the donkey with his sword drawn.

It was amazing to Jesus how, when Yahweh opened someone's eyes and they beheld the truth, they confessed their sins and transgressions.

Jesus reasoned with himself as he walked along with his mother, *What will it take to get mankind to open their own eyes and see the truth that is right in front of them? If only they would believe before Yahweh had to actually manifest himself before mankind.*

"What are you thinking, my son? You have not said a word for many hours, and I was beginning to think you had second thoughts about this visit."

Jesus thought to himself, *Mother, if you only knew what I now know.*

"Nothing much," responded Jesus. "Just wondering what mankind is waiting for to understand that Yahweh only wants the best for his creation and is waiting for the correct time for them to understand."

Mary smiled as they walked along, wondering how and why a young man of thirteen would be thinking of such deep thoughts. This was thoughts that high priests in the temple and learned scribes struggled over ever since the days of Abraham and the conquest of the promised land.

Even the great thinkers and prophets like Isaiah, Daniel, Jeremiah, and even King Solomon had struggled with this thought.

Isn't it said in their writings in the scrolls that were handed down through ages? thought Mary.

Then a thought came to Mary as she comforted Jesus. King Solomon, one of our ancestors, wrote, "Vanity, vanity, all in life is vanity" (Ecclesiastes 1:23). The caravan had come to a stop, and the master indicated it was time to make camp for the night.

After a full day's walk, both she and Jesus were ready for a meal and some sleep.

Jesus took charge of setting up the tent while Mary readied the evening meal.

After evening prayers and meal, the camp was cleaned up in preparation for the morning meal.

As the evening sun was setting, Mary noticed Jesus walking away from the camp. Mary wondered about this trait of Jesus as she had seen him do it a lot since he had turned twelve years old.

Just before the lights of the camp were lowered for the night, Jesus came back to the tent and kissed his mother on the head, preparing for bed.

Mary asked Jesus, "May I ask you a question? What were you doing out there alone?"

Jesus smiled and responded to her question, "Mother, I was talking to my Father in heaven."

Mary looked at her son. Surprised, she said, "Jesus, you know your father is in Nazareth with the other children."

Jesus said, "Yes, Mother, my earthly father is in Nazareth, but my Father in heaven is sitting on his throne."

Mary paused for a moment and realized just what Jesus had indicated by his statement.

Smiling as only a loving mother could, she said, "Good night, Jesus. Sleep soundly."

Mary had anything but a sound sleep that night. She was fretting about the things she did not know and could not reason out for herself.

During the night, in her sleep, an angel of the Lord came to her in her dreams, saying, "Blessed mother of the Messiah, do not worry yourself over Jesus's path and the things that cannot be fathomed by mere moral men.

"Jesus's time has not come, and the angels of heaven are watching over him. You will be blessed, but after his time has come, you will be pierced by a sword through your own heart" (Luke 2:35).

The angel departed Mary's dream, and she fell into a deep sleep, comforted by the vision but also troubled about her part in the vision.

The next morning, Jesus was up before dawn, readying the donkey and cart for the day's journey.

Mary came out of her tent thinking to build up the fire for the morning meal, but Jesus had already gotten things in order for the meal and his mother.

"Mother, did you sleep well?" Jesus indicated that he had slept well and rested.

Mary said she had also slept well and she had dreamed of her son.

Later that morning, as the caravan progressed along the trail, Mary took time to tell Jesus of her trip to Elizabeth's before he and John were born.

Mary told young Jesus how the trip to see Elizabeth was uneventful and she was glad that Yahweh had been with her on the journey.

As she finished her story of the trip, she heard Jesus utter something under his breath and asked what he had said.

Jesus looked up at his mother and spoke, "Yes, Mother, I know of your trip, for I was with you. I know, as you entered cousin Elizabeth's threshold, John jumped in Elizabeth's womb" (Luke 1:44).

Mary thought to herself, *I must have told him this story before,* but in her heart, she knew he knew.

*****

As the day grew long, noon came and went with the travelers eating their noon meal from prepared supplies they carried with them.

Mary watched Jesus interact with the other children and wondered where he could get all the energy he displayed throughout the day.

With the trail becoming more uneven and the shadows of the hills growing long, Mary called to Jesus to be vigilant to his surroundings as the caravan had left the flatlands and was beginning to enter the dangerous area that robbers and thieves dwelled.

Then the caravan began to slow, and the shout went up to slow the animals and carts. Jesus ran on ahead of his mother to see the excitement that had rippled through the lines of people.

When Jesus finally reached the head of the lead wagon, he spied a man lying on the side of the road on the opposite side. He lay some distance from the caravan.

From what Jesus could see, the man was almost naked, blooded, and not moving (Luke 1:44).

As Jesus looked on this poor man, he saw a number of priests and scribes and godly men walk up to the man on the ground, look at him, and turn their backs. One scribe saw the man and crossed over to the other side of the road without looking at him again.

Now Jesus, seeing this, wondered to himself, *Why are these godly men not offering help?*

With this, Jesus said very lowly, "Father, someone should help this poor man as he is one of our neighbors also. Father, I know you hear me, and I thank you for this" (John 11:42).

CHAPTER 5

THE GOOD SAMARITAN

WHEN THE CARAVAN'S ANIMALS and travelers settled down to witness the event on the other side of the road, a finely dressed man, from Jesus's perspective, led his donkey out of the caravan's line and crossed the road to where the half-naked man lay.

As the man approached the injured man, he bent down with a cloth and jug of water and began to administer to the injuries of the man.

Everyone in the caravan by now was watching and whispering to themselves, "That man is a Samaritan. What is he doing helping a Jew?"

After the man tended to the Jew's injuries, he helped the injured man to his feet and put him on his donkey and brought him back into the line of the caravan so they could continue on their way.

In a few hours, the caravan drew near a town with an inn.

The Samaritan led the donkey out of the line and to the door of the inn and helped the injured man off and into the inn.

A few minutes later, the finely dressed Samaritan came back out and returned to his place in the caravan, and they continued on until it was time to make camp.

*****

After Jesus helped his mother set up their camp for the night, Jesus was unusually quiet and did not engage his mother in talk as he normally did.

Mary noticed that, during evening prayers, Jesus had seemed far away as he gave thanks to Yahweh for all things.

Once the evening meal was finished and everything had been put away for the night, Jesus asked his mother, "Mother, would it be all right if I walked around a little bit before bed?"

"Of course," Mary told him. "Just don't bother any other people."

"I will not, Mother, without their permission."

Jesus found the Samaritan man a few yards from their own tent and donkey.

"Mister, sir, may I talk to you for a few minutes?"

The man, taken aback by the question of a young man, indicated it would be all right.

As Jesus sat down next to the campfire, he felt the man was studying him and probably thinking, *Now what would, or could, a young man, especially a young Jew, want to ask me?*

"What can I answer for you, my young master?"

Young Jesus asked, "If I may, why did you help the man on the side of the road this afternoon?"

The man gave a little laugh and said, "What would you have done in my place?"

Jesus said, "If I had had the means to help him, I would have helped him!"

The Samaritan said, "Of course, you would have, for the injured man was a Jew also like yourself."

25

Jesus looked at the man with understanding far beyond his age and said, "But, sir, you are a Samaritan, and Jews and Samaritan have no dealings with each other" (John 4:9c).

"Ah," said the man, "but even your laws say we are to care and love our neighbors. So how do we know who our neighbors are unless we love and care for each other!"

"Sir," asked Jesus, "did you just leave the man at the inn, and is that as far as your care went?"

The man smiled at Jesus and said, "No, it isn't. If a man asks for your cloak, offer your tunic also. In this case, I told the innkeeper to take care of the injured man and give him what he needs, and when I return, I will pay for the costs. And if there is anything else he needs, get it, and I will pay for it when I come this way."

Jesus thanked the man for his time and set off toward his mother's tent.

CHAPTER 6

THE ARRIVAL

WHEN JOHN SAT DOWN at the table for the morning meal, his mother asked, "What do you plan on doing today, John?"

John thought for a moment and replied, "I think today I will go and try and find some honey for us to have when Mary and Jesus get here."

Elizabeth smiled and said, "You know they may not be here until just before the Sabbath."

John looked at her and said, "Mother, they will here today," and continued eating his food.

Elizabeth was cleaning up the table as she saw John leaving out the front gate with a clean pail in his hand for the honey.

She offered a small prayer to El Shaddai to watch over John and keep him safe from harm.

*****

Elizabeth was hanging out the freshly washed laundry in the heat of the day.

She heard John come running though the vineyard hollering, "They are here. They're coming. Mother! They are coming!"

Elizabeth dropped the tunic she had in her hand into the wash basket and looked up to see John coming through the garden gate.

"Mother," John said, "Jesus and Mary are coming."

Elizabeth looked down the path toward where someone had to travel to come to the house but could not see anyone.

"How do you know, John?" she asked.

"I just know," answered John. "I can tell they are just around the bend in the road."

His mother looked down the road again and said yes. She could see Mary and Jesus leading the cart and donkey.

Elizabeth thought, *I wonder how John knew they were just that close?*

"John, go put the bucket of honey in the kitchen and clean yourself up for them to see you."

But John had already started for the house.

When Mary, Jesus, and the donkey and cart got close to the house, they could see John and his mother standing in the yard and waving to get their attention.

Mary thought, *Praise be to Yahweh for seeing us through this trip.*

It had been a trying three days for Mary. The trip, being sure Jesus was safe and all, went well. The questions about all she had heard still lingered with her, as well as questions that only Joseph would be able to answer. But she put them out of her mind and just wanted to rest and spend time with Elizabeth, talking about their two sons, who seemed to have a lot in common.

She felt, with Elizabeth's blessings, it would be an early day for her and not necessarily for Jesus.

Elizabeth started the evening meal for the four of them, and when Mary wanted to help, Elizabeth would not let her.

Elizabeth told Mary that she had invited Mary and Jesus and they were the guests as Elizabeth had invited them.

It was getting near the twelfth hour when the prayers were said by John and Jesus, and they all sat down for the evening meal.

"What do you boys plan to do tomorrow?" asked John's mother.

John looked up and told his mother they had planned to go fishing in the nearby lake.

"Well, just be careful, and if you catch anything, be sure to bring it home so we can have something besides lamb or goat to eat," said Elizabeth.

So the day had been set for them, and Elizabeth suggested she and Mary go to the market to buy some fresh vegetables while the boys were gone.

CHAPTER 7

THE FISHING TRIP

"**C**OME ON, JESUS!" JOHN exclaimed. "We will miss the best time to fish."

Jesus, still tired from the three days' journey, rolled over and said to John, "The fish will wait for us. Have no fear. We will get some fish for supper."

John rolled his eyes and straightened up his bed so his mother or Mary would not have to do it.

John was at the table eating his food as Jesus walked out of the bedroom and into the kitchen area.

"John," Jesus said, "the day is long, and we have plenty of time to get there."

John again rolled his eyes and said, "Jesus, you do not understand. We must first find bait to fish with."

Jesus laughed and said, "Yahweh will provide fishing bait for us."

John looked at Jesus and said, "Oh sure, we will just stumble over it on the way to lake!"

"Of course, we will," interjected Jesus. "Yahweh will provide!"

Mary, as she prepared the lunch for the boys, was listening to the banter between the boys.

She thought to herself, *How unsure John is, but how convinced Jesus is that everything will be provided for them. How different these two boys are from each other, but how utterly similar they are.*

She took the knapsack she had prepared with the bread, figs, grapes, and cheese and set it on the table between the two boys.

"John, Jesus, listen to me," said Mary. "Be careful when you are near the water and look out for each other. Now be on your way and walk carefully on your trip."

With a kiss for their mothers, they picked up the knapsack, grabbed the fishing poles, and departed the house and yard.

Elizabeth glanced at Mary and told her not to worry, for John had been to the lake to fish many times.

Mary smiled at Elizabeth and acknowledged her statement and said, "Oh, I'm not worried, Elizabeth, for Yahweh is with both of them, and the angels will watch over them until their time comes."

As John and Jesus walked through the small vineyard that Zechariah had planted many years ago, the boys' hearts were light and carefree, anticipating the coming day and all it held for them.

John turned to Jesus and said, "Jesus, have you ever had the feeling that there was someone watching you no matter where you were going or what you were doing?"

Jesus picked up a stone and tossed it away and said to John, "Yes, John, I have. But we, you and I, must always be alert for the things that Yahweh sends our way to help guide us and direct us.

"John, there are many things in the scrolls that foretell of the coming Messiah that the priests and scribes do not understand. They were told to our ancestors to let them know that there will come a time when the Israelites will welcome the Messiah but reject him. It is foretold in Isaiah and Jeremiah, but the priests and scribes can only see what they want to see.

"They are like whitewashed tombs, clean on the outside but dry as bones on the inside. Yahweh sent you and I to make them realize that all men are children of God, all the way back to our ancestor, the first man, Adam.

"Truly I say to you, John, that all we talk about and you witness must be kept to ourselves until you and my time comes as directed by Yahweh's spirit."

Just then, they had cleared the vineyard, and the path opened into a large grassy field.

As they walked along, grasshoppers started jumping in front of them, landing on their heads, tunics, and clothes.

"Hurry, grab them!" shouted John. "They will make excellent bait."

Jesus thought to himself, *Yahweh provided. Thank you, Father, for hearing my prayer. Praise to your name!*

John had taken his hat off and was putting the grasshoppers in it.

"John," Jesus said, "that should be enough as they will provide enough bait that we will need."

John gathered up his hat and pole along with the knapsack that held their lunch. "Well, Jesus, let's be off to the lake to catch some fish."

When they reached the lake, they started looking for a spot that looked like it would produce fish.

Upon finding a spot that John liked, they settled down and started fishing.

Conversations between young men, especially these two young men, varied greatly and covered a variety of topics. Many topics, if had been viewed by learned men, would have seemed deep and thought provoking; but to Jesus and John, they were as if these were everyday occurrences and things they thought about all the time.

"Oh no!" said John.

Jesus turned to see John's fishing line wrapped around a small tree in the water.

John was pulling on the line and about to break it; so Jesus said, "Stop, John, I will retrieve it for you."

John said, "Jesus, the water is too deep to wade out to the place it is wrapped around."

Jesus smiled, stepped off the bank, and walked the twelve or fifteen feet to where the tree was and unhooked it. He then turned around and walked back to the bank.

Sitting down, Jesus said, "Let's eat and talk, John. I am hungry."

*****

John sat there transfixed on Jesus with his mouth agape and unable to speak. "Surely, Jesus, you are the son of Yahweh. Praise your name."

Jesus looked at John and said, "Verily, verily I say to you, John. These and many more signs will be shown to you before our time comes, but we are not to say or do anything that will squelch the Holy Spirit's guidance. Truly I say to you. These things will come again to our recollection when the Holy Spirit and Yahweh deems it so.

"John, there will come a time when we are persecuted in the Father's name by men who are blind to the light of the world."

Jesus looked at John and said, "John, did you realize who I am?"

"No, Jesus," said John. "It was revealed to me through the spirit that talks to me when I pray."

"Blessed are you, John, for as the Scriptures say, you will be a voice crying in the wilderness to prepare the way for the Messiah."

As John looked up, a fishing boat that had been in the middle of the lake drifted closer to shore on their side of the lake.

John said to Jesus, "Look. They have been fishing since we have been here, and there has not been any activity on the boat."

Jesus said, "They have no faith that they can catch fish here or that there is any fish in this lake." Jesus stood up and said in a quiet voice, "Oh, ye of little fate." Then Jesus called out to the master of the boat, "Sir, have you caught any fish today?"

The master of the boat called back to Jesus, "No, young master. We have been fishing since the early hours and only have a few fish to show for our work."

Jesus called back, "Take your nets and put them over on the other side of your boat."

The master of the boat said to himself, *What does this young boy know about fishing?*

One of the other boat hands, who was the boat master's son, said, "Father, what could it hurt?"

With that, the master of the boat told his crew to do as the young man said.

As soon as the nets were let down, almost immediately the boat heaved to that side and the net straightened out, ready to burst with fish.

"Help me, sons!" hollered the boat master. "We have many fish in the nets, and we need to get them into the boat."

With the boat master's two sons and a third crew member, he started hauling on the net.

As the crew worked on the net, the boat drifted closer to the bank where John and Jesus stood.

When all the fish had been gathered in, the master of the boat asked, "What is your name, young master?"

Jesus answered, "I am known as Jesus of Nazareth, son of Joseph the carpenter, and this is John, son of Zechariah, the temple priest. May I ask your name, kind sir?"

"Of course."

But Jesus already knew who this boat master was.

"My name is Zebedee, and these are my sons, James and John." Zebedee asked, "Do you and your cousin have enough fish to take home to your mothers? If not, we now have more than we really need, so you are welcome to all you want."

Jesus thanked Zebedee and started walking toward the boat. As the sun was beginning to go down behind the clouds, he pretended to step on rocks in the water so as not to expose his true nature.

"Master," Zebedee said with concern, "be careful, young master, or you will slip into the water."

As Jesus approached the boat, he directed his speech to the young sons of Zebedee and exclaimed, "You fish well, James and John, but one day soon, you will become fishers of men!"

Zebedee handed the fish in a bag and wished Jesus and John a safe trip home and that Yahweh watch over them.

CHAPTER 8

TIME OF LEARNING

WHEN JESUS AND JOHN returned home with the fish Zebedee had given them, Mary and Elizabeth were surprised at the number and size of the fish.

Mary exclaimed, "Oh my! We all will have to pitch in to get the fish cleaned and salted so they will keep for us to eat."

Even though the boys were tired, they set out to help Mary and Elizabeth with the task of cleaning and preserving the catch.

As the cleaning process progressed, idle chatter between all four of them was lighthearted and robust.

Mary asked Jesus who had caught the most fish and who had caught the largest and if he enjoyed the fishing.

Jesus said he did enjoy the fishing trip and about meeting Zebedee and his sons, James and John, and how the fishermen had caught a large number of fish and had offered some to John and Jesus to take home to their mothers.

Mary thought for a moment and read between the lines what Jesus was saying.

"John," asked his mother, Elizabeth, "have you seen this boat before on the lake?"

John thought for a moment and said he had thought he had seen it, but the master and his sons looked familiar to him.

He believed he had seen them in town inquiring about buying a new fishing boat, and John had heard they were from the Galilee area.

He told his mother he thought the master and his sons were from the Capernaum area or Magadan although John wasn't really sure.

The cleaning completed. Mary insisted the two boys go and get washed up before they eat their supper and then get ready for bed after evening prayers.

Like two young deer, the boys bounded off outside to wash up, change clothes, and make ready for their prayers.

In deep thought about the day's events, John said he would pour the water over Jesus first so he could clean himself first.

Jesus said, "No, John. I have come to serve, not to be served. Let me be the one to pour first. I can wait for you to finish.

With some laughing and kidding, the boys got cleaned and dressed to present themselves to their mothers before prayers.

Elizabeth and Mary were listening with intent interest at all the laughter and joking they did.

When the boys came back into the house, Mary said, "You two must have had a really good time today."

Upon which, John remarked, "Oh, cousin Mary, we had a wonderful time, and I shall not forget this day."

"Mother?" Jesus asked, "Is it all right if I go outside for a few minutes alone?"

Mary looked at Elizabeth and said, "Yes, Jesus, but don't be long."

"I will not," remarked Jesus.

When Jesus left the house to find a secluded area, Elizabeth asked Mary, "Is he all right?"

"Yes," answered Mary. "He has been doing this occasionally since he was twelve, just before we went to the Passover festival in Jerusalem."

Elizabeth looked puzzled but accepted Mary's explanation and said, "It must help him sleep at night."

Mary said, "So it seems."

The next day, being the sixth day of the week and the day of "preparation," Mary and Elizabeth busied themselves with the chores that needed to be done before the Sabbath began at sundown.

As the sun was setting behind the hills, Elizabeth, Mary, Jesus, and John traveled to the synagogue to attend the Sabbath services.

Jesus and John went to the main worship area and were seated. Elizabeth and Mary climbed the small staircase to the upper area where the women worshipped from.

Jesus watched his mother and Elizabeth ascend the staircase and thought, *Yes, Father, as you will, one day, we will worship all together in one place and come to you just as we are.*

The rabbi of the synagogue got up and praised Yahweh and said his worship prayer.

When he was finished and lighted the candles, he said, "We are fortunate. We have a young man visiting from Nazareth by the name of Jesus. Could we get him to come up and read from the scroll of his choice?"

Jesus, perplexed but not surprised or ashamed, got up and walked to the front of the congregation.

Selecting a scroll of Isaiah, Jesus began to read although he hardly looked at the scroll as he recited the words written by the prophet.

Ho, everyone who thirsts, come to the waters,
and you who have no money, come, buy and eat.
Come, buy and eat.
Yes, come buy wine and milk without
money and without price.
Why do you spend money for what is not
bread?
And your wages for what does not satisfy?
Listen carefully to me and eat what is good.

And let your soul delight itself in abundance. (Isaiah 55:1–3)

While Jesus read from Isaiah, Mary and Elizabeth watched and listened to Jesus very carefully.

When Jesus had finished, Elizabeth turned to Mary; and under her breath, she whispered, "Mary, he hardly looked at the scroll as he read."

Mary smiled and said, "Yes, isn't it wonderful that he knows the Holy Scriptures as well as he does?"

Elizabeth said, "I am sure his father is very proud of him."

When the service was completed, the two mothers joined their sons on the steps of the synagogue where the rabbi was talking to Jesus and John.

"You, young man, have a very good grasp of the Holy Scriptures. Do you study the scrolls very often?"

Jesus looked at the old rabbi and said, "Master, I have been in God's Word all my life, and I'm pleased you see that the Word is true."

The short walk back to the house was quiet between Mary and Elizabeth, but the two boys ran ahead of their mothers, as most young boys will do.

John asked Jesus, "What did the Scriptures mean when you read, 'Buy bread and wine with no money'?"

Jesus looked at John and said, "Truly I tell you, John, that the Messiah will offer to anyone who believes life-giving water and bread to sustain their spiritual lives.

"It will not cost even one minute's wage to those who only believe that the Messiah offers life-giving words.

"Verily, verily I tell you, John. When men are thirsting for the living water I offer and bread to sustain their lives, they will be able to come and partake of the banquet the Father offers without it costing them any money other than to worship him who is in heaven, the One who sent you and I."

CHAPTER 9

THE PRINCE OF THE AIR

THE SABBATH CAME AND went for the family, with Jesus and John studying the scrolls, and since Jesus and John were alone, Jesus interpreted some of the scriptures John did not understand.

There were many scriptures that spoke of the coming Messiah and what he would mean to the world and some that were frightening to John as they spoke of serpents, monsters, and the things that were foretold of coming events.

John asked a number of times, "How do you know if these things are true?"

Jesus looked at John and told him that everything in the scrolls were inspired by Yahweh to the prophets and could be believed (2 Timothy 3:16).

Jesus was waiting for John to ask the question that was on John's thoughts.

Finally John asked, "Jesus, I know that I must play a part in this, but I do not understand how I am to precede the Messiah?"

Jesus turned to the scroll of Deuteronomy and read to John:

> The Lord Your God will raise up for you a prophet
> like me [Moses] from your midst, from your

brethren. Him you shall hear. (Deuteronomy 18:15)

Then Jesus turned to Isaiah again and read:

> Therefore the Lord Himself will give you a sign: Behold, the virgin shall conceive and bear a son, and shall call His name Immanuel, which means "God is with us." (Isaiah 7:14)

Then Jesus turned to Isaiah and read again:

> For unto us a child is born, unto us a Son is given, and the government will be upon His shoulder.
> And His name will be Wonderful Counselor, Mighty God, Everlasting Father, Prince of Peace.
> His government and peace there will be no end.
> Upon the throne of David and over his kingdom.
> To order it and establish it with judgement and justice, from that time forward even forever.
> The zeal of the Lord of Host will perform this. (Isaiah 9:6–7)

"Verily, verily I say to you, John. God the Father has sent you and me to open the eyes of the children of Israel."

"But what does that have to do to do with me, Jesus?" asked John.

"Here, let me show you in scripture, John."

"In Isaiah, the prophet writes, 'Behold the voice of one crying in the wilderness: prepare the way of the Lord, make straight in the desert, a highway for our God'" (Isaiah 40:3).

John looked at Jesus and blinked his eyes. "What does that have to do with me?" he asked.

Jesus said, "John, think back about your own birth. Cousin Elizabeth was beyond childbearing age, and your father was beyond age to be able to conceive. But your mother prayed to Yahweh for it to happen, and it did.

"Didn't Zechariah say an angel appeared to him in the temple and told him he was to conceive a child through Elizabeth? (Luke 1:13)

"Even so much as to bind his mouth shut until your birth because your father had doubts" (Luke 1:20).

Jesus rolled the scroll up and tied it with a ribbon and placed it back into its rightful place in the scroll box.

"John, we must pray to the Father for guidance in his will for us, for there is no other way."

After prayer time, thanking the Father for all he had done for them, they reentered the living area and kissed their mothers and started to bed.

Mary asked Jesus, "Are you not going to seek a quiet place tonight?"

Jesus said, "Not tonight, Mother. Both John and I have talked to Father."

So off the bed the boys went.

The next morning, as it was the first day of the new week, Elizabeth had started working to make new cheese and grinding wheat to make bread.

Mary was doing the washing and catching up on the housework that had gone undone over the Sabbath.

Elizabeth called to John, "John, please come here. I have need of you to make a trip to town to buy some things at the market."

"Oh, good!" cried John as he punched Jesus in the shoulder. "We're getting to go to town!"

"Now, John, here is the money to buy the lintels, pomegranates, and a bag of wheat grain. Also, there is something extra for you and Jesus to buy a stick of honey candy."

So off the two boys went with a warning from Elizabeth to be careful in town as there were stories of a band of boys bothering the townspeople.

"We'll be careful!" hollered John as they went around the bend in the road.

As they walked along, the two boys discussed things they had talked about on the Sabbath and what might mean to each one of them individually; then in the pathway, John saw a rabbit lying still and not moving.

John looked at Jesus and said, "It must be dead as it is not moving or trying to run away."

Jesus went over to the dead animal and picked it up in in his hands.

"No, John," Jesus said. "I believe it is only stunned."

But Jesus knew the rabbit was dead as he saw blood in its ear as if it had been hit with a stone from a sling.

Jesus cradled the rabbit in his hands and arms and looked to the sky and closed his eyes softly.

John watched Jesus and saw him move his lips but could not hear the words Jesus said.

Then Jesus knelt down and put the rabbit on the ground on all four feet.

The rabbit looked around and then looked at Jesus and hopped away.

"There," said Jesus, "he is better now!"

The boys continued on their way until they came to the town and the market.

Since it was midmorning, the market was bustling and crowed with shoppers from all over the area.

John, being the son of the temple priest, was welcomed by everyone whom they saw. John introduced most of them to his cousin Jesus and informed them Jesus was from Nazareth.

During this time of the first-century Judea, Nazareth was a crossroads of any people and characters, some not very savory people.

Some who met John and Jesus said behind the boys' backs, "Can anything good come from Nazareth?" (John 1:46).

Of course, Jesus heard them but thought it better to turn the other cheek and say a gentle word and not cause wrath.

The boys mingled with the market shoppers and saw Zebedee and his sons selling their fish and spoke to them.

They purchased the items Elizabeth had sent them after and had enough money to buy the honey stick she said they could buy.

While wandering around, a band of tough-looking boys, a little older than John and Jesus, were watching their activities.

One tough-looking boy, a little older than John, said to his friends, "Let's wait until they get out of town, and then we will rob them."

But little did Barabbas know or perceive that Jesus knew his heart and his evil intentions toward John and Jesus.

When the hour grew late, just after the ninth hour, the boys finished their shopping and started home from the marketplace.

When John and Jesus had rounded a bend in the road, there stood the four boys and Barabus in the middle of the road.

John said, "Jesus, we are in trouble."

Jesus told John to act like there was nothing to fear and keep walking and that Yahweh was with them.

When John and Jesus got close to the band of boys, Barabus said, "Give us your wares, and we will leave you alone."

Jesus stepped in front of John and walked up to Barabus, looked him in the eye, and laid his hand on Barabus's shoulder.

As Barabus flinched, Jesus said something; but John could not hear it but heard a voice say, "Leave us alone, O Son of the Most High Yahweh. We have nothing to do with you."

Jesus then said so John could hear him, "Be gone from these children of Yahweh, and do not bother them again."

The boys, all five of them, fell to the ground, got up, and acted dazed and stupefied.

Jesus told them to be on their way and pray to Yahweh when they got home.

*****

The shadows were getting longer as the sun dipped behind the some of the hills surrounding their path home.

As they switched hands holding the market items, they talked in hushed tones about the events of the day.

John asked Jesus, "What happened to the five boys that stood in the way on the road?"

Jesus scuffled his sandals at some hill of dirt left by a cartwheel and said, "Truly I tell you, John. It is not flesh and blood that man fights but the prince of the air and his demons" (Ephesians 6:12).

As they walked and talked, John was thinking about all the bad things he had seen men do to each other, to their animals, and even to themselves since he had been old enough to understand cruelty in men.

Jesus was walking and thinking also about the day's activities and was saying a small prayer to the Father, "Father, thank you for hearing me, for I know you always hear me. As you have told me long ago, the evil one will come at me whenever he can, and I must be on alert for his spirits."

John inquired, "How do we know it is the evil one's spirits, Jesus?"

"John," Jesus said, "a long time ago, when Yahweh created the heavens and earth with his word, Lucifer was Yahweh's next in command of the angels.

"He was a glorious sight, the shining one. He reigned over the angels in heaven and directed the heavenly chorus. Yahweh favored him so much earth was created for him to have dominion over.

"When Yahweh formed mankind in Yahweh's image and placed him in the garden with the man's helper, Lucifer became jealous, and his pride caused him to sin against the Father and all that was in heaven.

"As it is written in Isaiah's scroll,

Oh, how you have fallen from heaven, oh, Lucifer, son of the morning!

How you are cut down to the ground, you who weakened the nations!

For you have said in your heart, 'I will ascend to the heavens, I will exalt my throne above the stars of Yahweh! I will also sit on the mount of the congregation on the farthest sides of the North. I will ascend above the heights of the clouds. I will be like the Most High!'" (Isaiah 14:12–14)

This was a lot for John to comprehend, so Jesus stopped for a few minutes until John asked, "Jesus, how did the evil one get down here on earth?"

Jesus continued, "John, there was a great battle in heaven between Yahweh's angels led by Michael and Gabriel, the two archangels, and one-third of the angels that followed Lucifer."

"Yahweh had given the earth to Lucifer, and Yahweh did not change his mind no matter what may have unfolded.

"So Lucifer and his demons rule the air and attack all that Yahweh has created. The evil one cannot attack Father directly, so he attacks Father's greatest creation, mankind."

John looked at Jesus as they walked and started to say something, then John said, "There is home, and Mother and Mary are in the yard waiting for us. I sure am hungry. I hope they have the evening meal prepared."

Jesus laughed a little chuckle and said, "John, we do not live by bread alone but by the very word of Yahweh!"

*****

After the boys had reached the house and greeted their mothers, they said their evening prayers and sat down for the evening meal.

During the meal, Mary and Elizabeth inquired if all had gone well with their trip to the market in town and whom they had seen and talked to during the day.

"Did Jesus enjoy meeting the people that mingled in the marketplace?"

"John," Jesus said, "introduced me to a whole lot of people, and we saw the master of the boat Zebedee and his sons."

John was about to speak up concerning the band of boys that were possessed; but Jesus, anticipating John's story, spoke up and cut John off.

"Yes, Mother, all went according to Yahweh's will, and it was uneventful for us."

"Praise Yahweh," said Elizabeth. "I was so concerned that you two might be confronted by the band of boys that was roaming the town. I had heard they could have robbed some travelers from a far country."

John took up Jesus's thoughts not to reveal any of the signs he had seen in Jesus's company.

"No, Mother," interjected John, "all went well according to Yahweh's will."

The family completed the meal in silence after that, and the boys retired to wash up and change for bed.

The next day, as it was the day of preparation before the Sabbath day, Elizabeth had the boys busy getting milk from the goat for cheese and grinding wheat kernels for flour.

John asked Jesus, "What would you like to do, milk the goat or grind the wheat for flour?"

Jesus said, "John, whichever you do, I will do the other!"

The rest of the day went pretty much like this, with Jesus and John joking and bantering with each other while obeying their mothers' wishes.

The day came and went with all going according to Elizabeth's plans.

Mother Mary had been quiet during the evening meal.

Jesus asked, "Mother, are you all right this evening?"

"Yes," replied Mary. "I have been thinking about your father, Joseph, and how he is doing as we have been gone for some time and I am sure he is worried about you and me."

Jesus looked up from his plate and, with a very solemn face, said, "Mother, that is what Yahweh wants. Father Joseph is to watch over us until my time comes."

Elizabeth looked at Mary with a puzzled face and smiled as only a knowing mother could.

The Sabbath came and went, as well as the next two weeks with John and Jesus playing, fishing, and interacting with some of the other children in the surrounding homes.

The bond between Jesus and John had become very strong and was growing stronger day by day.

The preparation day before the last Sabbath they were to spend with Elizabeth and John, Mary told Jesus that they would begin their journey home on the first day of the week.

Jesus looked at John and told his mother, "As you wish, Mother."

That evening, after evening meal and prayers, John and Jesus were in their room talking while lying on their pallets on the floor when Jesus said to John, "Truly I tell you, John. This is the last time we shall meet until my time has come and you have started preaching the coming of the Messiah and the Father's kingdom. We must deliver the message the Father wants us to preach, which is to repent of man's sinful ways and obey his word."

John asked, "How will I know when that time comes?"

Jesus answered him, "John, the spirit of Yahweh will envelop you and give you the words you are to deliver!"

*****

After the Sabbath day had ended, John helped Jesus pack all the belongings and gifts that Elizabeth had somehow kept hidden from Mary and Jesus.

There were new prayer shawls for the male members of the family and a new tunic for Simone.

Along with these gifts, Elizabeth had put in Mary's purse a small bag of coins to buy whatever Mary thought they would need on the journey home.

Mary tried to return the coins, but Elizabeth knew of the plight of a carpenter. So when Mary tried to return the coins, Elizabeth refused to take the coins.

The Romans had levied a harsh tax on the people of Judea, so Elizabeth understood the need in Joseph's family.

Joseph could use the extra money, especially with all of Joseph's children.

After all, it was only she, Zechariah, and John. And with Zechariah's income from the temple and vineyard, they had plenty to share with Mary and Joseph.

Things were not so good in Nazareth as in Judea, so work for Joseph would be slow from now on until the planting season.

Elizabeth told Mary, "Shh, you will need the money later if you and Jesus do not need it on the journey home!"

After prayers that night, everyone was eager to go to bed.

*****

The next morning, dawn came early for the two women and the boys. As they ate their morning meal, not much was said to each other.

John and Jesus picked at each other, with the two mothers admonishing them in a good-hearted manner.

John went out to hitch up the donkey to the cart and make sure all was secure in the cart along with the feed for the donkey.

Now Mary and Jesus were ready to be off to Nazareth.

CHAPTER 10

THE RETURN HOME

WHEN THE CARAVAN STARTED moving, Mary, Jesus, and the donkey with the cart fell in line with the other travelers.

As they walked along, Mary watched Jesus as he walked beside the donkey, holding the rope tied to the halter.

Somehow Jesus looked either taller or more mature for his age than when they first made the trip to Elizabeth's house.

"I bet Father Joseph will be glad to see us when we reach Nazareth in a couple of days," said Mary.

Jesus thought for a few minutes and said, "Mother, will James ever come to see me as a friend?"

Mary thought this odd for Jesus to ask her. "What do you mean?"

"Well, sometimes when he and I are together, he will accuse me of being different than the other children in Nazareth. This sometimes hurts me, and I want to defend myself and explain what you and I know to be the truth."

Mary looked at her son and, with a hurt in her heart, said to Jesus, "Jesus, your father, Joseph, knows you, and I am sure he has told James and the other children all they need to know and that

Yahweh understands the doubts they must have concerning you and his plans for you.

"In time, it will come to pass, Yahweh willing. They will see the plans he has for each one of us, including your brother James."

The journey to Nazareth went well for Mary and Jesus, with Jesus talking to the children and adults alike, inquiring about their lives and losses they had endured during their lives.

At the evening meal, Mary would inquire about what Jesus had been doing and how he was holding up on the trip.

The last night they were on the trail, they had camped out just thirty or so miles from the disbanding location.

That evening, as Mary and Jesus sat and ate their meal, Mary inquired of Jesus, "Jesus, you have been quiet these past couple of hours. Is there anything a mother can do for you?"

"No, Mother," answered Jesus. "You are doing and have been doing all Yahweh is requiring you to do."

Then Mary answered, "What seems to be bothering you this evening?"

"Mother," came Jesus's reply, "I see so much hurt and chaos in the world, and mankind has seemed to have lost their way and will to carry on. The children I have talked to have the spirit of Yahweh, but it seems to be crushed under the weight of the world's trials. That spirit must be reinstated to the place Yahweh intended it to be in all mankind.

"It seems, as the children grow older, a dark cloud descends over their spirit, and only by them being obedient to Yahweh will he be able to defend them from the evil one. That is Yahweh's only desire for mankind. He owns all things, and there is nothing man can offer Yahweh on the altar of worship he does not own.

"He wants only for mankind to worship Him. As it is written in the Psalms."

Come, let us bow down in worship,
Let us kneel before the Lord our Maker;
for He is our God
and we are the people of His pasture,
the flock under His care. (Psalm 95:6–7)

Mary pondered in her heart these things Jesus said.

As Jesus rose to go off to his quiet place, Mary reassured him as only a loving mother could, "All in due time, son. Yahweh will see to it."

*****

The next morning was a hurried, busy time for all of the travelers. Mary and Jesus were no exception.

With anticipation of arriving home after such a long time, Mary was anxious to get home to see Joseph and the children.

"Hurry, Jesus," cried Mary. "We must get the donkey hitched and the cart ready to get in line of the caravan."

"Yes, Mother," Jesus said as he finished with the bridle and halter of the donkey.

The last hour of their trip seemed like an eternity to Mary, but Jesus was obedient and walked alone ahead of the donkey and cart, seemingly in his own world.

When they walked up in front of the house, Joseph came out with the children to welcome Mary and Jesus home.

"How are you, my wife?" Joseph asked.

"I am fine, husband. How are you doing, my husband?" Mary smiled and said she was well and the trip had been uneventful.

Then Joseph turned toward Jesus and asked him if all was well with his son.

"Yes, Father," answered Jesus. "We had a wonderful trip and saw many wonderful things in Judah."

"And how is Elizabeth, Zechariah, and John?"

Mary answered, "They are fine and doing well, but we did not get to see Zechariah as he was at the temple in Jerusalem."

Joseph stepped aside and said to his children, "Welcome your mother and brother."

James, the eldest, hugged Mary and welcomed her home but did not say anything to Jesus.

Likewise, each of the children welcomed Mary and Jesus home.

Simone hugged Jesus and asked if he was all right and that she had missed him while they were away.

"James!" said Joseph. "Welcome your bother home from the trip."

As James started to walk away, he mumbled something under his breath that no one heard except Jesus, "He is not my brother. He was gone having a good time with Mary, and I was having to do my job and his also. It was not fair!"

James turned and looked at Jesus staring at him, and he was embarrassed for himself.

As James approached Jesus, he told him, "Welcome home."

Jesus said, "Thank you, James. There will soon come a time when you will thank me and the Father."

The children took the gifts and other things given to them from Elizabeth and John into the house while James took the donkey and cart to the corral, unhooked and fed the donkey, and went into the house for the evening meal.

PART 2

AD 14-16

Judah–Nazareth

CHAPTER 11

THE POLITICAL CHANGE

I N AD 14, TIBERIUS, emperor of all of Rome, succeeded Caesar Augustus.

With the coming of Tiberius, so came changes in the political atmosphere of the Judahian leadership in Jerusalem and the temple priests.

Pontius Pilate was installed as procurator of Judah, and the temple authorities were also changed (Hubers History).

Throughout all of Judah, the climate of the Jews' well-being started being infringed on by both the Roman authorities and the temple priests. The Sanhedrin and Sadducees grew powerful and more vocal into the everyday life of the Jewish citizens of Judah.

When Joseph Caiaphas was appointed high priest by the procurator Valerius Gratus and was acting as the official, he had the backing of Annas, who was an ex officio high priest and very influential.

There seemed to be a sweeping movement among the scribes, priests, and the Sanhedrin to appease the Roman authorities, who had installed Herod Antipas as tetrarch of Galilee and Perea.

When the temple priest met with the ruling Sanhedrin, the discussion was about who would support the authority set forth by Caiaphas and backed up by Annas.

*****

Judah, home of Zechariah, Elizabeth, and John, who by now was eighteen years of age

"Mother!" exclaimed John. "Something has been bothering me for the longest time, and I was wondering if you could or father could shed some light or understanding on this for me?"

"What is it, John?" asked his mother.

"Mother, you know the story that Joseph and Mary had to take Jesus and flee to Egypt to evade Herod the Great's decree to kill all the infants in Judah?" (Matthew 2:13).

"Yes, son," answered his mother.

"Well, Mother, both Jesus and I are about the same age."

"Yes," Elizabeth said, "you are six months older than Jesus."

"Well," asked John, "where did we escape to, to escape the decree Herod had put out in Judah, as you and father were living there?"

Elizabeth wondered when John might ask this question as it was common knowledge among the family of Zechariah and Elizabeth's family and especially the temple people.

"John, sit down, and I will explain this story for you as it is part of the plan of Yahweh.

"After about two years of both your and Jesus's births, a group of eastern princes came to Jerusalem, seeking the 'new king of Israel.' Herod gathered his wise men of the court and inquired about such a birth in Judahian territory. The wise men of Herod's court consulted the ancient scrolls and found in the scroll of Micah where it was foretold.

> But you Bethlehem Ephrathah, though you are little among the thousands of Judah, yet out of you shall come forth to me, the one to be ruler

56

in Israel whose going forth are from of old, from everlasting to everlasting. (Micah 5:1)

"When Herod heard this scripture and the court magician's interpretation indicating a king was born that was to take his place on the throne of Judah, Herod flew into a rage and wanted the eastern princes to find the 'new king.'

"The wise princes found Jesus, Mary, and Joseph in Bethlehem in a stable at an inn, for there was no room there for them because of the census that Caesar Augustus had decreed to be taken in Judah.

"The eastern princes left gifts befitting a king with Mary and Joseph for Jesus. The princes return to their own lands by a different route so King Herod could not find them as the princes perceived that King Herod wanted to rid the land of this child who might be a threat to the Herod household and his throne.

King Herod had decreed for his army to go into Judah and slaughter all male children two years of age and younger. (Matthew 2:16)

"Your cousin Mary told us an angel appeared to Joseph in a dream warning him of the impending massacre and told Joseph to take Mary and the child to Egypt until they were summoned to return to Israel. It is Yahweh's plans for events to happen, and the gifts the magi gave to Jesus helped Mary and Joseph to make the necessary trip.

"Now for your question, John. At the same time, the angel that warned Joseph also appeared to your father, warning him also.

"The angel told Zechariah to take me and you to the hill county in Judah so we could be hidden from Herod's army (The Protoevangelium Gospel 16:3).

"Some of the temple priests and their families in that region befriended us and hid us among their own people, hills, and secluded villages. When we heard that Herod the Great had died, we returned to Judah and continued our lives.

"One fact that has been hidden for all these years is that, when Herod could not find your father and you, he had his army go to the temple and kill the first old priest his army could find and told his people that Zechariah was killed.

"Now, John, you really know what happened so long ago in Bethlehem."

"Mother," asked John, "what did Joseph do with his children when he and Mary Jesus traveled to Egypt?"

"Ah," said Elizabeth, "that is a clever question of you to ask.

"When Caesar decreed the census be taken, Joseph's first wife had died, and Joseph sent the children to his mother- and father-in-law to watch over them until the decreed census was over. When they returned and settled in Nazareth, Joseph and Mary went for James and Simone and brought them back to Nazareth from Cana."

*****

Later on that week, John was coming out of his room wearing the camel-hide coat the "neighbor" had given him so many years ago.

"John!" exclaimed his mother. "Do you still have the coat?"

John looked down at the coat vest and said, "Yes, Mother. It still fits and has not deteriorated any from when the neighbor gave it to me. I saw no reason to throw it away as it was a gift and I can still use it."

Elizabeth walked over to her son, felt the coat vest, and marveled at how soft and pliable the material was.

"Well, if you like it and it serves a purpose, then I see no reason to throw it away either," said Elizabeth.

John thanked his mother and told her he had planned to go to town and see if he could do some work for some of the merchants that were in the marketplace.

Elizabeth said, "John, could you please pick some melons for us? Here is some money to buy them with."

With that, John went out the door and headed to town, tucking the coins in his waistband.

*****

Nazareth

"Father," inquired Jesus, "have you always wanted to be a carpenter?"

Joseph looked at his son of eighteen and wondered where this questioning was leading.

"Yes," answered Joseph. "My father taught me, and his father taught him. It has been this way for many years."

Jesus thought for a moment and replied, "Do you think it is all right if a son did not want to follow in his father's footsteps?"

"Of course, my son. It is for every man to find his own calling and not necessary for a son to follow in his father's vocation. We must follow how the spirit of Yahweh leads us, and with the spirit's guidance, we will find our own way in life. Why do you ask, Jesus?"

"I was just wondering," replied Jesus. "Cousin John's father is a temple priest, and what if John did not want to be a priest in the confines of a temple or synagogue but maybe out in the open space doing Yahweh's work there?"

Joseph smiled at himself and said, "Jesus, John would still be doing as his father, Zechariah, but just not in a temple, but all the same, it would be in Yahweh's interest and glory."

Jesus said, "Yes, Father, you are correct. We can worship Yahweh any place and not just in a temple and anytime."

As Simone busied herself with the preparation of the evening meal, she talked to Mary.

"Mother Mary, the children in the town talk about Jesus being strange or different because of the things he says."

Mary, puzzled, asked, "What things, Simone?"

"Well, Mother, you know, like, he is always saying strange things about 'his Father in heaven' and doing things that I have never seen anyone else do."

"Such as?" asked Mary.

"Well, you know, the other day before the last Sabbath, some boys were playing on the roof of Jacob the farmer's house, you know, the one out by the outskirts of town. The boys were shoving and pushing each other, and I looked and saw Benjamin slip and fall to the ground. He did not move after hitting the ground really hard.

"Jesus walked over to him and laid his hands on Benjamine. Jesus looked up to the sky and said something I could not hear.

"When Jesus lowered his head, Benjamine opened his eyes and got up and walked off. (Infancy Gospel 19:3)

"Mother! I know Benjamine was hurt bad. He had to have been."

Mary put her arm around Simone and told her that there was a simple explanation to this although Mary did not explain.

Simone finished helping Mary and getting the table ready for the evening meal.

CHAPTER 12

THE PASSOVER FESTIVAL

Lazarus, Mary, and Martha

JOSEPH SAT AT THE table with Jesus, James, Joses, and Judas. Joseph said the prayer of grace and thanksgiving, then said to Mary, "We have had a good month of work in the shop and the market stall. Mary, do you think we are all ready to take the annual trip to Jerusalem for the Passover?"

Mary looked up from her place at the adjacent table with Simone and winked at her daughter. "Yes, my husband. With the new cart and a little preparation, we can be ready by the new week. The new cart you and Jesus made, we should be able to put all we need for the trip. It will be good to see Elizabeth, John, and Zechariah again!"

"Well then, it is done!" said Joseph. "We will finish what we have to do in the carpenter shop and try and sell what is left to sell in the market stall and ready ourselves for the journey."

The boys, as if one, said, "Yes, Father."

*****

As John came in from the trip into town for his mother, he saw Elizabeth sitting at the table weeping.

"Mother, what is wrong?"

Elizabeth told her son to sit down and listen very carefully. "You know your father has been at the temple in Jerusalem. Now, John, your father was old and had lived a wonderful life."

John interrupted his mother and said, "Mother, what are you talking about? 'Had lived'? Has father passed?"

"Yes," wept Elizabeth, "on his way home from the temple. A messenger just before you came to our house and brought the bad news into this household. The messenger brought the message and a scroll with all of your father's belongings, as well as Zechariah's donkey."

"John, through tears in his eyes, saw the scroll and unrolled it so it spread out in front of him and his mother.

Priest Zechariah,

You have been a wonderful servant of the Most High Yahweh, and because of this service, we are granting you a pension as you retire from active priesthood.

May Yahweh grant you good health and place you in His holy hands forevermore!

Signed,
Joseph Caiaphas
High Priest, Temple of Jerusalem

John sat there stunned and staring at the scroll. "Is that all, Mother? Is that all they had to say for a priest who served twenty years, serving Yahweh and doing the bidding of the temple? Those bunch of vipers," spat John. "Their day is coming soon, and the wrath of Yahweh will be upon them.

"Where is Father's body, Mother?" asked John.

"They took it back to Jerusalem to get it ready to bury before the Passover.

"John," said Elizabeth, "we will go and attend to your father's things and stay over for the Passover at my sister's house."

John, the ever-obedient son that he was, spoke in hushed tones and said, "Yes, Mother, as you wish."

*****

Jerusalem in AD 15 was a city of some one million people and, during Passover week, swelled to well over one and one-half to two million people.

Mostly there were devoted Jews and worshippers of Yahweh, but as in all cultures and societies, there were those that chose to prey on other's weakness and frailties.

One such person was Judas Iscariot.

Judas thought that manipulating people and getting what he wanted was a lot better than having to toil and sweat for one's daily bread.

He was always on the lookout for anyone or anything he could manipulate to make his way in the world easier.

"Over here, James," called Joseph to his son. "This looks like a good spot for us to set up camp. There is water nearby and plenty of firewood for us to use."

James led the donkeys that were yoked together over to the spot Joseph had indicated.

As Jesus started undoing the harness and yoke straps, he was looking around at all the other camps, tents, and throngs of people.

"There sure is a lot of people this year," said Jesus. "It seems to grow each year."

"Yes," said Mary. "When you were but a child, after coming from Egypt, we were able to camp within the walls of the city."

"Oh, yes," interjected James, "I do remember that!"

After all the tents and camping gear were unloaded and the cart and donkeys secured with a chain, the children were eager to run around and find their friends.

James and Jesus hung back to help Joseph set up the two tents—one for Mary, Joseph, and Simone and the other larger tent for the four boys.

After this had been done, Mary asked Joseph if it would be all right if James and Jesus walked around and visited others if they so wanted.

Joseph said, "Of course, it is all right. Just be back before evening meal."

Both boys agreed and set off, each going his own way.

*****

"Peace be with you, brother."

Lazarus walked up to Jesus and asked, "Where are you from, sir?"

Jesus responded, "From Nazareth. I am Jesus, son of Joseph the carpenter, and who might you be, brother?"

Lazarus looked at his two sisters, who were one and two years younger than he. Lazarus said, "I am Lazarus, and these are my two sisters, Mary and Martha."

Jesus looked at the sisters and said, "Peace be with you, sisters, and may Yahweh in heaven give you peace."

Lazarus spoke up and asked Jesus if he had been coming to the Passover before this year.

Jesus said, "Yes, for a very long time."

He had been celebrating Passover but did not go into just how long.

Lazarus said, "I had just wondered as we have never seen you before. We used to come with our parents, but they passed away right after last year's Passover, and we decided to come by ourselves this year as our home is in Bethany and is only two miles away toward the Salt Sea" (Dead Sea).

Jesus felt a kinship with the trio and the ease that they showed in speaking with Jesus.

Jesus said his farewell to Lazarus, Mary, and Martha and told them he would be around the area most of the week for them to seek him out.

As Lazarus and his sisters turned to leave and go to their own camp and tents, Mary, youngest of the two sisters, said, "There is something about that Jesus that I like" (song "There's Something about That Name").

The other two agreed and said they would try and keep his company as much as they could.

The next day came and went, with Mary, mother of Jesus; Joseph; and the three youngest children going to the marketplace and shopping for supplies they needed.

Jesus and James started out together but soon drifted apart, each pursuing his own course.

When Jesus stepped into the temple gates, he witnessed a sight that turned his blood cold.

There in the middle of the temple court were money changers, animal sellers for sacrifice, and food vendors.

Jesus said slowly, "Father, they have turned your temple into a den of thieves and scoundrels."

He inquired from a man whose name was Nicodemus, a member of the Sanhedrin.

As Jesus talked to Nicodemus, Nicodemus told him he had only been a member of the Sanhedrin since the priest Zechariah, who had retired, died.

Jesus hung his head and said a soft prayer for Elizabeth and John.

Upon raising his head, Jesus asked Nicodemus when the courtyard had been turned into a money-changer chamber.

Nicodemus said, "Oh, my young master, by the order of Caiaphas, the high priest of the temple. He decreed it last year when he was appointed high priest by the procurator Valerius Gratus to help add to the temple treasury." But Nicodemus added, "I do not abide in this outrage, and I am only one small voice. I believe the money is flowing into other purses."

Jesus said, "I am sure you are correct, kind sir, and peace be with you and your family."

Nicodemus likewise thanked Jesus and was on his way.

*****

During the meal that evening, Jesus asked his father, Joseph, why such was done in the temple.

Joseph told Jesus that, after it had come to pass that the temple authorities were collecting money this way by charging Passover goers for the sacrificial animals, they could not only probably line their own pockets but appease the Roman authorities by paying for some of the costs of housing the legions of soldiers in Jerusalem.

James, listening to the conversation between his father and Jesus, said, "Jesus, what business is that of yours? We live in Nazareth and are far from Jerusalem and Roman rule!"

Jesus said, "Matter of fact, James, there will come a time when their authority will reach over all the known world, and when that happens, it will be the end of times. (Matthew 24)

"Brother will be against brother. Men will be lovers of men as was in the time of Sodom and Gomorrah, and the pursuit of money will be the end of mankind. We all must be vigilant to the plight of our brother and his welfare. If we do not love one another, then who will love us as mankind?"

James looked at Jesus and said, "I just do not believe you. Yahweh will not let the world end because he made us in his image and loves us to not do that!"

Jesus smiled and said, "James, one day, your eyes will see the light of the world, and you will worship as you have never worshipped before. I tell you the truth. As was in the days of Noah, so shall man see the signs before the end-times.

"Mother, Father, I met a new member of the Sanhedrin today. He said he had only been selected as a member because the priest Zechariah had been retired and then, on his way home to Judah, died en route."

Mary looked at Joseph and said, "Oh, poor Elizabeth and John. Whatever will they do?"

Jesus told his mother, "Do not be anxious, Mother, for they will be taken care of!"

Mary said, "How do you know this, Jesus?"

His reply was one she did not expect. "I know the Father will take care of them, Mother!"

James, always the unbeliever, just rolled his eyes and shook his head.

Simone said in a low voice, "See what I said, Mother?"

Everyone at that point became quiet and finished their meal.

CHAPTER 13

ELIZABETH'S SISTER

J OSEPH WAS UP AT the crack of dawn as was his normal habit. As he got the fire going for the morning meal, James and Jesus came out of the boys' tent, talking as only two brothers could.

James said, "Jesus, I do not know what you are talking about. Every time we get into a discussion of the law, you throw something into the conversation that makes no sense to me."

As James walked off, Jesus looked at James and told him he would eventually see what the true light of the world was.

Joseph looked at Jesus and said, "Son, leave him be. When the true time comes for him to see, he will see!"

"But, Father!" Jesus said. "I am only trying to guide him as the Father in heaven directs me."

"I know, Jesus, but we must give James time to come to his own realization of the truth."

"I know, Father Joseph, but I so want James to love me as I love him. That is all I ask."

Mary had come out of the tent with Simone right behind her. "Husband Joseph," she said, "if I could get your permission, I would like to go into Jerusalem to find where Elizabeth's sister lives and see if Elizabeth is still there. She had given me the address when Jesus and I were visiting her a while back, and I am still concerned with her and John's well-being."

Joseph smiled and thought, *After all these years, Mary is still the obedient wife, and I praise Yahweh for this woman.*

"Yes, Mary, you have my permission, but do you think you can find the address?"

Mary held out a piece of parchment with the address and detailed instructions on how to find the address.

"Very well. Will Simone be going with you?"

"Yes," replied Mary. "I would very much like Elizabeth to meet Simone." And in reply to Joseph, Mary asked, "What is to become of Joses and Judas?"

"I will let them go with me as I go in between campsites to see if there is any repair work I can do for the other travelers," answered Joseph. "They are old enough to start helping me."

In a little while, Mary and Simone started out toward the Eastern Gate of Jerusalem to seek the address Elizabeth had given Mary.

As they walked among Passover visitors, Mary pointed out places to Simone, such as the temple, the women's court, the court of gentiles, and then the residential homes that continued as far as Simone could see. Among these homes lay Elizabeth's sister's home.

"Ah, here it is," remarked Mary as they looked at the house.

Mary and Simone stepped up to the three steps that led to the front door of the house and knocked on the doorframe.

They waited for a few minutes. When no one came to the door, Mary turned to move away, but the door opened.

A lady that just had to be Elizabeth's sister said, "Yes, may I help you?"

Mary cleared her voice and said, "Is this the address of the sister of Elizabeth, Zechariah the priest's wife?"

The lady said, "And you must be Mary, mother of Jesus and wife of Joseph!"

Mary was a bit taken aback by the introduction but took it in stride. "Yes, I am, and this is Simone, daughter of my husband, Joseph."

About that time, Elizabeth was pushing her sister and hugged Mary and Simone. "Praise Yahweh," said Elizabeth. I have so been thinking about you, Mary, and Yahweh has answered my prayers."

After they all had gotten comfortable in the sitting room and Abigail had served tea and pastries, she formally introduced herself to Mary and Simone.

Elizabeth had married Zechariah when he was a new priest in the temple. Abigale had been a handmaiden at the temple in Jerusalem, serving the high priest and doing the necessary things that were needed to be done in and around the temple.

When Caiaphas had been installed by the procurator Valerius Gratus, by virtue of Abigale's relation to Zechariah, she also was retired with a pension.

The older woman marveled at Simone's beauty and her pose and manners.

Of course, being a young woman, Simone blushed and thanked them for their generosity.

Mary spoke up, "Elizabeth, what are you and John going to do now that Zechariah is gone?"

Elizabeth looked at Abigale and said, "Since Zechariah is gone, there is no reason for me to go back to Judah and the lonely house! John has gone down to sell the house and property and will bring the proceeds back to me.

"In so doing, I will give him what he wants of the money, and Abigale has invited me to live here with her so we can be closer together.

"John has indicated he is called to do Yahweh's bidding in the desert. There is no need for him to stay in Judah. The fishing has fallen off as the Jordan River has rerouted its bed after the last flood and the lake that was there has been closed off by the course of the river. And the fishermen have migrated back to Galilee, so he is going to the desert to seek his way."

"Well," said Mary, "Simone, your father and brothers are probably wondering where we are this late in the day," as it was way past the noon hour.

Abigale loaded up a basket with pastries and bread and gave it to Simone. "Here, take this to your father and brothers, and Yahweh's blessings be with you," said Abigale.

Mary and Simone thanked their cousin and Abigale and started back on their way to the camp near the Mount of Olives.

It was close to the twelfth hour when Mary and Simone arrived at the camp.

All four boys and Joseph were there anticipating Mary and Simone's return.

Mary thought to herself, *At least they could have started the evening meal,* as she and Simone approached the camp.

How surprised she was when Joseph kissed her on her cheek and let her know the meal had been fixed and ready to eat.

Praise Yahweh, thought Mary, and she smiled.

****

Jesus was up and tending to the children while James helped Joseph with odds and ends around the campsite. Simone was busying herself with the preparation of the morning meal.

"What, may I ask, are you children going to do today?" Mary asked.

Jesus thought for a moment and answered his mother, "Mother, I am going to the marketplace and walk around to meet people from other areas of Judah and beyond."

James stood up from a squatting position and said, "Mother, I plan to go to see the wizards and magicians in the marketplace. There is a man there that others say can fly or hover off the ground."

Jesus looked at his father and said, "James! Do not yoke yourself with such people, for they are the adversary of the Father in heaven!"

With the meal finished, the children helped Simone clean up, and James and Jesus headed for the east gate of the Jerusalem wall.

Simone took the other two boys walking around the area, and she had told her mother she planned to take the boys walking around to the garden of Gethsemane on the Mount of Olives.

Mary looked at her husband and inquired of him, "What, may I ask, are you going to do today, husband?"

Joseph smiled and said, "Since all are gone from the camp, I plan to spend some time with my wife, which I do not get to do at home."

Mary smiled and laughed, "Oh, Joseph! Did you also bring her along with us?"

Joseph smiled and closed his eyes, leaned back on his pallet, and thought, *How great is Yahweh!*

*****

Jesus walked alongside James and talked to his half brother.

"James, be careful of such people in your life. What they believe and do not believe could have an impact on your thoughts about what is right and what is wrong in Yahweh's eyes.

"As we walk along on our life's journey, we will find that the road to the Father's kingdom is very narrow and hard to walk by ourselves. That is why we rely on Yahweh's guidance and word to see us through all the trials and tribulations that we face in our daily lives.

"James, I want you to remember this, that the wicked one comes dressed in all types of disguises and will place obstacles in your path. Do not be deceived. Yahweh will not be mocked.

"He who sows to the flesh will reap the fresh, but he who sows to the spirit of Yahweh will reap the spirit" (Galatians 6:7–9).

Just as they split their journey up, James said, "As you say, Jesus."

CHAPTER 14

THE MARKETPLACE

EVEN THOUGH JAMES HAD walked on ahead of him, Jesus kept his eyes on James progressing through the throng of people.

Finally James was diverted from the place to where wizards were plying their trade. Jesus looked where James had been looking and saw a young girl about James's age.

Jesus smiled and offered a small prayer the Yahweh would protect James, for Yahweh had plans for James in the grand scheme of things.

Jesus stopped by a few vendors' tents and stalls in the marketplace before continuing on in his walk.

"Hello, Jesus," came a small female voice.

Jesus turned and saw Martha and Mary standing there.

"Peace be with you and peace to you," offered Jesus.

"Peace be with you, Jesus," said Martha.

"Where is your brother?" inquired Jesus.

"He is over by the silversmiths looking at some things he was interested in. He will be along soon."

"When Martha and I saw you walking in the marketplace, we told Lazarus we would come and get you. He told us he would join us soon." Then she turned to see Lazarus walking their way.

n, Jesus sensed eyes on him and the three

joined his sisters and Jesus, Jesus turned and
ut Jesus's age looking at them.

t to himself, *Hello, Judas Iscariot. I was wondering
d appear. But, Judas, it is way too early as my time has
e*, thought Jesus.

the four of them talked and walked along, Jesus could sense
s walking their way.

When Judas got within speaking distance, Jesus turned and said, "Welcome, brother. Peace and Yahweh's blessings be with you!"

Judas was taken aback a bit as he did not expect such a greeting.

"Can we help you?" inquired Jesus.

"I did not mean to startle you as I did. I have been seeing you around the marketplace, and since you are not from Jerusalem, I thought I could be of help to you with any Passover items you might need. The Sabbath day is coming soon, and you might need some things."

Jesus smiled and told Judas that they were not in need of anything at the moment but, if he would like, he could walk along with them.

Judas saw an opportunity to get to know these four as it might come in handy later on.

Judas saw the adornment and accessories that Mary wore and thought to himself, *These are people I need to become better acquainted with, for it might come in handy later on.*

Greed is a demon that comes on a little at a time. When we least expect it, greed turns into lust, not necessary for man or woman, but lust for things that we do not have or need; and that becomes covetousness.

As the day wore on, the five of them walked and talked about all the changes that were taking place in Jerusalem and Judah—the changing of the temple's high priest, Herod Antipas being installed as tetrarch of Galilee and Perea, and a new procurator of Jerusalem by the name of Pontius Pilate.

On a dark note, Lazarus said, "I do not see why the Romans have started crucifying criminals on a cross!"

At this, Jesus quoted the scrolls from Deuteronomy:

> If man has committed a sin deserving of death, and he is put to death and you hang him on a tree [the cross was sometimes called a tree], his body shall not remain overnight on the tree, but you shall surely bury him that day so that you do not defile the land which the Lord Yahweh is giving you as an inheritance; for he who is hanged is accursed of Yahweh. (Deuteronomy 21:22–23)

Jesus went on to explain this scripture to the four followers.

"The Romans viewed crucifixion as the worst kind of humiliation that mankind can suffer. Truly I tell you. The cross will one day be a sign of Yahweh's triumph over evil and death!" explained Jesus.

It was nearing the sixth hour, and Martha spoke up, "It is almost the noon hour. Let us stop and buy lunch for us all, and we can continue on our walk later on."

Jesus spoke up and said, "I do not have any funds to buy such food."

Martha looked at Lazarus and said, "We can share the cost of our daily bread, brother. Be our guests. You also, Judas."

Jesus walked over to a shady place under a tree and sat down on the ground with Judas and Lazarus while Mary and Martha went to buy cheese, figs, and fruit. On the way from the food stand, Mary went to draw a jug of cool water for them all.

As they sat, the men together and the two sisters off to one side, Jesus said a thanksgiving prayer for all Yahweh had done for them.

Jesus looked at each one and said, "Truly, I tell you, we do live by bread alone but the very word of Yahweh" (Matthew 1:4).

The day was drawing to a close all too quickly for Lazarus and his sisters.

Judas had endured the talk and was trying to gather as much information from them as best he could.

He understood the brother and sisters were from Bethany, a small hamlet two miles from Jerusalem near the foothills leading to the Dead Sea.

Evidently their parents had been fairly rich and had died a year earlier, leaving the children a house and some wealth.

But this other person, this Jesus, was hard for Judas to figure out.

Jesus claimed to be the son of a carpenter from Nazareth, but Judas thought Jesus sounded like a preacher or prophet or both. He was not really sure.

Judas thought to himself, *He is one I must pay attention to and watch closely.*

Judas was deep in thought as Jesus talked to Lazarus and his sisters.

"Judas!" said Jesus. "We are talking about what the Romans were doing, and what are your thoughts on this?"

Judas, thinking, said, "It really does not concern me. They are the authorities until the Messiah comes and overthrows them. Then we shall see them take their belongings and return to Rome." Judas then asked, "Jesus, do you believe that the Messiah will come as a great warrior and rid Israel of this plague?"

Jesus thought and said, "That is what the temple priests are teaching."

"He shall come as a mighty warrior and lead his people out of bondage, just as Moses did in Egypt," said Judas.

Jesus smiled and said so everyone could hear him and discern what he was saying to them, "Truly I tell you. The Messiah will come as an unblemished lamb to be brought to the slaughter for the sins of the world" (Zephaniah 1:7–8).

"But," said Mary, "how shall the Messiah be able to save us if he is slaughtered for mankind's sins?"

"Verily, verily I tell you, Mary. Without the Messiah being sacrificed, man cannot find salvation.

"When Cain, the first man's son, slew his brother, Abel, Yahweh foresaw man's inherent evil established when the evil one tempted our mother and the first man, Adam, in the garden.

"Since that time, Yahweh has deemed it necessary to send his Son, the Messiah, to give the people an example of how to live and treat his brother and sister and be a sacrifice for them.

"For the second great commandment is as the first. 'They shall love thy neighbor as thyself, just as you love Yahweh, with all your heart, all your soul, and all your might'" (Leviticus 19:18).

With this, Jesus bid his farewell to the others, "Peace be with you, and Yahweh's grace and mercy follow you all the days of your lives."

"And to you," they all said in unison.

"Judas," Jesus called, "if I could speak with you for a time."

Judas hung back as the others departed, going their own way.

"Judas," Jesus said, "we shall part for now, but very soon, we will meet again under very different circumstances. I tell you. Be very careful about yourself as I see the evil one sending his demons to attack you and dwell in you!"

Judas looked at Jesus and turned and walked away without saying another word.

Jesus then said, "You will have a choice to make, and your very life and mine will be at stake."

When Jesus reentered the marketplace, he spied a young woman standing over a man on the ground backed up onto a building wall.

"Will you please get up and come home with me, husband?"

The young man, a few years older than Jesus, replied, "Why should I, wife? I am no good as a husband to you. You deserve children, and I am unable to fulfill my responsibilities to you. I am cursed by Yahweh, and my fatherhood cannot come to light" (Infancy Gospel 7:2).

Jesus stepped closer to the couple and interjected, "Kind sir, do you love your wife and have been faithful to her through your vows?"

The man looked up at Jesus, puzzled, and said, "Yes, master. I have been doing all the scrolls tell me to do toward my wife and household. We have tried for oh so many years and have not been able to conceive a male child or even a female child. We do not really care as long as Yahweh would bless our house."

Jesus looked at the wife of the man and asked, "Is this so?"

The young woman said, "Yes, master, he has been very faithful husband since we were married, but this curse hangs over us."

Jesus bowed his head, looked to the sky, and said, "Holy Father, I stand in the gap for these two children, asking you to grant their petition and supplications! Father, I know you hear me, your Son, and I am thankful for all you do for your children."

With that, Jesus opened his eyes, smiled at the couple, and said, "Couple, go home as your petitions have been answered!"

*****

Jesus turned and walked farther into the marketplace and saw James waiting for him by the Eastern Gate.

"Hello, brother!" shouted James. "It is time for us to be going to the campsite."

With that, the two half brothers headed back to the valley and the others.

The next day was the day of preparation for Passover and everyone in the camp, Kidron Valley, and the Mount of Olives.

Mary had sent Simone, Jesus, and James to the market to purchase fresh fruit, goat's milk, and bread for the Sabbath's meals.

The meals had to be prepared in advance of the Sabbath according to the Law of Moses.

James was muttering to himself as they walked along, really paying no attention to the direction they were going.

"I wonder why," said James, "we cannot cook meals on the Sabbath for our own nourishment? After all, that is really not work."

"James," interjected Jesus, with Simone listening, "because that was the day that Yahweh rested after creating the heavens and earth, and he wants mankind to rest from all their toils during the week. It is a show of respect for the one who created life and gave us all that is on the earth. He wants us to be happy, but he also knows that we must rest and honor him as our Creator, James!

"That is all he really wants from us, our dedicated love and respect, and he will love us with his agape love."

James kept on walking and said under his breath, "Oh, Father, here we go again."

Jesus heard James's exclamation and said, "James, not far in the future, you will come to see the way, the truth, and the light that is all around you if you will open your eyes and hear with your ears."

CHAPTER 15

THE MIRACLE BEFORE
THE SABBATH

WHEN THE NOON HOUR had come and gone and the meal was over, Mary found the firewood, and water was low to be able to carry the family through the Sabbath day and into the first day of the week.

"James! Jesus! Please go and get some more firewood and water to carry us through to the new week."

The two young men headed off toward the creek's well and the woodpile by the Kidron creek.

As they walked along, James asked Jesus, "What would you like to do, brother? The firewood or the water?"

Jesus told his brother, "Whichever you choose to do, I will do the other."

James said, "Then, brother, I will gather the firewood, and you can draw the water from the well."

With that said, Jesus took the water jogs and headed toward the well, and James went toward the woodpile, next to the Kidron stream.

Just as Jesus had gotten a few steps on his way, he heard James holler, "I've been bitten by a viper" (Infancy Gospels 19:1)!

Jesus turned and saw James standing, holding his right arm.

Jesus set his water jogs down and started running to where James was standing, bent over.

"Be still," said Jesus as he took James's arm in his right hand and put it under his own left arm so James could not see the wound the viper had inflicted on James's forearm. "Let me see it!" exclaimed Jesus.

Jesus stepped to the side of James to block his view of the bite.

As soon as Jesus touched the wound that was bleeding with his hand and fingers, the poison of the viper flowed back out of the puncture wound of the fangs, and the bleeding ceased to run.

Jesus turned around and said, "Praise Yahweh. Brother, you were fortunate. The viper did not break the skin of your arm!"

James, wild eyed, said, "Jesus, I could swear by Yahweh that the viper had bitten me!"

Jesus said, "Brother, feel fortunate that is not what happened."

James looked at his arm where the viper had struck him. The skin was clean and not swollen.

Jesus helped pick up the firewood for James, and they walked to where the jugs lay.

"James," said Jesus, "it would be best not to tell Mary about this event as there is no need to worry her. You know how she is about these things, and there would be no need for her to be anxious for nothing" (Philippians 4:6).

James looked at Jesus and told Jesus, "Yes, brother, it would be best."

*****

When the jugs were filled with fresh water, the brothers headed back to the campsite with Simone in tow.

As they got near the tents, the family were getting ready to go to the Sabbath services as the sun was almost down and they had to walk to the temple services.

"Hurry," said Mary, "we must be off to the temple for the Passover Sabbath."

As the family walked along toward the temple, Lazarus, Mary, and Martha saw Jesus and, they assumed, his family.

As the brother and his two sisters drew closer to Jesus and his family, Lazarus asked Jesus if he and his sisters could join them for the Sabbath services.

Jesus looked at Joseph and Mary, and they nodded their agreement.

"Father, Mother," said Jesus, "these are three of my friends. This is Lazarus, Mary, and Martha from Bethany near the Salt Sea."

Joseph said, "Welcome."

Mary said, "Welcome, young friends. We are glad to meet friends of Jesus. Come join us and walk to the temple with us."

They entered Jerusalem through the Eastern Gate, which was the closest to the temple.

Herod's temple
20 BC to AD 70

The family and friends approached the temple area and passed through the *Soreg* bordering the temple grounds.

As they passed through, they ascended the twelve steps leading to the Beautiful Gate and the temple terrace.

Mary took Simone by the hand, and Martha and Mary followed her to the court of women in the center of the temple grounds.

Joseph told James, Jesus, Joses, and Judas (not Judas Iscariot) to follow him to the men's court overlooking the court of priests, where they would be able to see the activities of the high priest.

Mary called back to Joseph, "We will meet you back at the Beautiful Gate upon service ending!"

"Yes," answered Joseph.

Jesus was in thought as Joseph asked him, "Jesus, are you thinking of something?"

"I was thinking and pondering. Why do the husbands and wives not get to worship Yahweh together? He surely wants us to live in harmony and live together, so why cannot they worship as one?"

Joseph was perplexed at this question. "Jesus, I do not know why the law says that. Since our fathers came out of Egypt and the law was given to Moses in the desert, it has been this way."

Jesus thought to himself, *Yes, Father, it will change. With a lot of other things, your will be done!*

Although there were a lot of Sabbath goers at the temple, all went well, and everyone saw the services.

Judas, the youngest, was wondering about sacrifice when he asked Jesus, "Brother, why are they killing the cow and sheep?"

"Judas," Jesus said, "a long time ago, right after Yahweh created mankind and put him in the garden of Eden to have dominion over it and care for the animals, there, Yahweh gave Adam, the first man, and his helper, Eve, commandments. They could eat of anything in the garden but one tree, the tree of good and evil.

"The evil one, who had been one of Yahweh's angels, had rebelled and went against Yahweh's will. Yahweh cast the angel Lucifer out of the heavenly realm with one-third of the angels that followed Lucifer.

"In doing so, the evil one started attacking everything that Yahweh had created and entered the body of a serpent so he could deceive and attack Eve, the mother of us all. The serpent tricked Mother Eve into eating a fruit of the tree of good and evil against Yahweh's wishes.

"She also got the first man to eat also of the fruit. When they ate of the fruit, their eyes were opened, and they perceived they were naked and were ashamed.

"So they hid from Yahweh when he was walking in the cool of the evening time and could not find Adam or Eve.

"Yahweh called out, 'Where are you?'

"Adam said, 'I have heard your voice in the garden, and I was afraid because I was naked, and I hid myself.'

"Yahweh asked, 'Who told you, you were naked? Have you eaten from the tree of which I commanded you not to eat?' (Genesis 3:11)

"Then Adam blamed his helpmate, Eve, and Eve blamed the serpent. (Genesis 3:8–11)

"So Yahweh fashioned clothes out of an animal skin to make covering for Adam and Eve. The shedding of the animal blood represents the forgiveness of sins that man did.

"Yahweh forgave Adam and Eve, but because Yahweh's commandments were broken, Yahweh banished Adam and Eve from the garden and installed an angel there with a burning sword at the gate to guard it from others finding their way in."

Judas asked Jesus, "Is the location of the garden known to us?"

Jesus said, "No, Judas, but Yahweh has created a new kingdom for all who believe in him and the sacrifice he has sent to persuade man to believe."

With this explanation, Judas was quiet and watched the ritual taken place in the courtyard.

*****

When the services ended, Joseph, James, Jesus, and Judas, with Lazarus, walked to the area of the Beautiful Gate and waited until Mary and the sisters, along with Simone, found them.

As Lazarus walked beside Jesus, with his sisters next to him, he said, "On the morrow, Jesus, we will return to Bethany and our home."

"So be it," Jesus offered. "Lazarus," said Jesus, looking at him and his sisters, "Yahweh bless you and keep you, and may he make his glory shine on you the rest of your days. Lazarus, this is not goodbye but just a parting for a while. We will meet again!"

He looked at Martha and Mary and smiled. "Sisters, many things will come to pass, and our journeys cross many times. But always remember me, and when you need my help, send word, and I will come."

The families parted ways at the Eastern Gate; and as they neared their campground, Jesus turned to his mother and said, "Mother, I must take a walk by myself for a little while."

Mary replied, "If you must, Jesus."

"Yes, Mother, I must," said Jesus.

*****

As Jesus walked toward the Mount of Olives and the garden there, he was in deep thought about the coming years, and John and Elizabeth crossed his mind.

He thought to himself, *John, the time for you is rapidly approaching. The Father will show you the sign for your ministry. Do not be afraid. Yahweh is with you, and the Holy Spirit will guide you on your way.*

Jesus climbed the fifty or so feet up the mountain and entered the garden of Gethsemane. As he walked among the olive trees and fauna, he felt a comforting feeling surrounding him.

He knelt down and started to pray.

"Father, who art in heaven, hollowed be thy name. Father, thank you for hearing my plea for James this day. You know his role to play as my role unfolds for mankind to see. Open his eyes when you deem it and guide him in his role after I am taken back to your side to sit on your left hand.

"Father, I stand in the gap for Judas Iscariot for his role in this. Thine will but your will be done on earth as it is in heaven."

CHAPTER 16

THE CALL OF JOHN

The area of Judah

"WELL, YOUNG JOHN, YOU have made a wonderful transaction for your mother, Elizabeth. She should be well pleased with the results of negotiating this deal for her."

Samuel, a wealthy farmer and landowner in the Judah area, was pleased that he could help John and Elizabeth; and besides, he got a grand piece of land with the deal.

He had always had visions of the land and vineyard Zechariah had planted. It had produced very fine grapes every harvest, and he envisioned expanding the yard to many more acres.

"John, please tell me why your father, Zechariah, did not expand the vineyard when he could?"

John shook Samuel's hand and said, "Father was old, Samuel, and his duties at the synagogue took him away, and his time was limited. His duties at the temple usually fell at harvest time, and they took up a great deal of his attention. Besides, Father was not really interested in the vineyard as a moneymaking project."

With that, John turned and led his donkey, loaded with the few belongings Elizabeth had left and a few of John's meager things, toward the road to Jerusalem.

As John walked down the path leading to the road to Jerusalem, he was concerned with the money Samuel had given him for the sale of the house, vineyard, and property.

Silently John said, *Father Yahweh, be with me and guide and direct and protect me while I journey to Jerusalem to give Mother the money for the sale.*

With about twenty miles to travel to Jerusalem, John knew he would have to spend one night on the road, if not two.

When the shadows grew long as the sun was setting, John came upon a small caravan traveling the same way as he.

The wagon at the end of the train was being led by a young man about John's age, and walking beside him was young woman.

John hailed them and asked if he could fall in line behind them.

"My name is John," said John.

"Of course, brother," came the reply. "We're traveling to Jerusalem to see our uncle who is a member of the Sanhedrin. My name is David, and my sister is Debra."

John thanked them and fell into line with them.

Finally the wagon caravan came to a stop for the night; and John, without a tent, made his camp a little farther from the brother and his sister. Normally tents are kept close to each other for protection, but in John's case, he wanted to keep his distance from others.

John staked his donkey to the ground and fed him some grain and hay and water John had packed for the trip.

Without a fire, John made a pallet on the ground and settled in for the evening.

"Hello, brother," came the call.

John raised his head up and pulled himself onto his side and saw David coming his way.

"Yes, David?" said John.

"I see you did not make a fire or have no tent."

John laughed a bit and said, "No, I really did not have room for a tent or many provisions, only enough for one night on the trail for my donkey and the things I am taking to my mother in Jerusalem."

"Oh," said David, "does she live in Jerusalem?"

John, being who he was, answered, "Yes. Since my father died, she has decided to live with her sister-in-law, and she has moved there. After my father died, Zechariah's sister had asked my mother to move in with her so they could be closer."

David insisted John pack his pallet up, get his donkey, and move closer to their own wagon and tent.

When John got everything moved, David offered John some food consisting of cheese, cold lamb slice, and figs.

Also his sister offered John a mug of wine. But John refused the wine, saying he must not drink wine because of his mother's vow at his birth.

John thanked David and Debra and returned to his pallet by his donkey.

When John lay down, he fell into a frightful sleep.

An angel appeared. "John, do not be alarmed. I have come from the Lord to give you a sign that your time has come. After tending to your mother's business in Jerusalem, the Holy Spirit will lead you into the desert to purify yourself so you can clear the way for the Messiah. You will know him by his light and word."

The angel disappeared into nothingness. John woke up with a start and looked around, and all was well in the camp.

The next morning, John had morning meal with David and Debra, and they got on the way afterward.

As they walked along, David asked John, "What did your father do, John?"

John told them that Zechariah had been a priest of the temple for twenty-something years and, when the new high priest started making changes in the temple, his father was retired and possibly that was one of the causes of his death.

David looked at John and said, "John, I am sorry for your loss. We understand our uncle Nicodemus replaced your father as a priest in the temple."

John looked at them and said, "Yahweh works in mysterious ways. We must be obedient to his will!"

"What do you plan to do, John, after you see your mother in Jerusalem?" asked David.

John said, "At present, I am led by the spirit of Yahweh and will obey the commands of Yahweh!"

CHAPTER 17

JOHN'S DEPARTING

Jerusalem, one day later

WHEN JOHN APPROACHED ABIGALE'S house, he was wondering how his mother will accept his calling from Yahweh.

He tied the donkey up to the hitching post next to the house. He had tribulations as to his mother's fears and concerns for him and the role Yahweh might have had for his ministry.

John leaned his staff next to the threshold of the door and rapped three hard times on the entryway.

Abigale opened the door, saw John standing there, and exclaimed, "Oh, praise Yahweh! Elizabeth, John has returned from Judah! Come in. Come in, nephew," said Abigale.

About the time John entered the small courtyard, Elizabeth came through the house door.

"Oh, praise Yahweh for your safe return, son, and I thank Yahweh for your safe return."

John looked at his mother and aunt and said, "Thank you both for your concern for my welfare. All is well with my soul and being."

Elizabeth thought for a moment at John's statement about his soul. This was the first time John had said anything really serious about his spiritual well-being.

"Come, let us take the things you carry, and you can rest your feet and body."

As the two women scurried around the house sorting out the items John had brought off the donkey, John sat down and retrieved the money pouch he had hidden in his waistband and set it on the floor next to him.

When Elizabeth and Abigale came back to the living area, John said, "Mother, here are the proceeds from the sale of the house, vineyard, and property in Judah. I was able to strike a fair bargain with Samuel of Judah. I was pleased, and he seemed to be also. I surely hope you are pleased."

As John walked to the table in the living area, he untied the purse strings and poured the contents on the table.

Elizabeth's eyes grew wide and was astonished at the site of all the money.

There on the table lay the coins John had received from Samuel—one hundred talents, which equaled to six hundred thousand denarii. A denarius equaled to one day's wages.

Abigale only stood there and stared at the money.

Elizabeth sat down in a chair and held her hand over her heart.

"John," said Elizabeth, "how in Yahweh's name did you strike such a deal with Samuel?"

"Mother, I do not know. I had told some merchants in town we were wanting to sell the house and land. The next day, Samuel showed up at the house, and we talked and discussed the property Father had left us. There really was no haggling. He offered me what you see, and since I thought it was a fair sum, we struck the deal," said John.

"Oh, son, it is more than enough, and I praise Yahweh for being with you."

"Mother, Samuel sent his blessing to you with this message."

Elizabeth, mother of John and wife of Zechariah,

Peace be with you, and may the angel of the
Lord watch over you the remainder of your life.

"Mother, it was all rather strange, but we know Yahweh moves in mysterious ways his wonders to perform. The wonders of Yahweh are not to be questioned."

"Yes, my son, so it shall be."

John went outside after gathering up the money, putting it back in the purse and handing it to his mother.

As he put the donkey in the pen behind the house, he wondered how his mother would react to his leaving her and Jerusalem.

John thought, *Surely this and much more is in Yahweh's hands.*

At the evening meal, after prayers, John decided he would tell his mother and Abigale he would be taking his leave of them.

During prayers, Elizabeth studied John as he prayed and thanked Yahweh for all he had given and done for them.

"John," asked his mother, "are you all right? Are you sick or something?"

John smiled and said, "No, Mother, I am well. There is something I need to discuss with you and Aunt Abigale."

Both of the women perked up, and Elizabeth said, "Yes, son?"

"Mother, on the way here from Judah, I was asleep on the trail when I had a vision. An angel of the Lord came to me and told me the time for my ministry had come and I am to pave the way for the Messiah."

Elizabeth's heart sank, for she knew in her heart of hearts this day was coming.

Abigale's heart also jumped in her chest as Elizabeth had confided in her sister-in-law of the birth announced to Zechariah and Elizabeth and the ramifications of the birth of John by the angel Gabriel.

Elizabeth told John, "Yes, my son, it is so ordained, and I knew this day was coming."

"What are you going to do?" asked Abigale.

"I am to follow the Holy Spirit to guide me into the desert in Judah, around the Jordan River, where the angels of the Lord will prepare me for my role Yahweh has set in motion."

They all set there in silence for a while until Elizabeth got up, went to John, hugged him, and kissed him on his head.

*****

The next morning, Elizabeth came to John and told him, "John, this is way too much money. I want you to have your share of it being the first and only son of your father."

John looked up at his mother and said, "Mother, I will not be needing the money you received, so it is to benefit you and Abigale if you so want. The Lord will provide for me, and I will want for nothing."

"Then, John, take the donkey and sell her to a merchant, and you take what you get for her," said Elizabeth.

John agreed to this concession of his mother's and started preparing to leave.

John put the bridle on the she-donkey and led her out of the pen and toward the Gennath Gate on the southern side of Jerusalem.

As he approached the gate, there was a young man pulling a cart of pottery.

And not too well either, thought John.

"Here, young man," said John. "I have no need of this she-donkey, and I see you could use her for your business."

The young man looked at John and said, "Sir, I have no money to buy her!"

John laughed and said, "Did I say anything about buying her? She is yours! Here."

The young man said, "Thank you, kind sir. Yahweh be praised for your kindness, and bless you forever."

With that said, John started walking, staff in hand, and smiled the smile of a man content in his life.

When John had passed through the Gennath Gate, he came to a place called Golgotha, or the place of the skull.

John walked by the hill. He got an ominous feeling and felt like a dark cloud had descended over him.

He kept walking in deep thought, and soon he was out of sight of Jerusalem and into the wilderness.

*****

Six months later
The house of Jacob and Leah, Jerusalem

She was standing in the kitchen fixing her husband's evening meal when Leah looked up to see Jacob coming through the door of the house.

"Oh, husband, I am so glad you are home early. Have you had a good day at the pottery shop?"

Jacob looked at his wife and said, "Yes, wife, it has been so much easier since that man gave me the she-donkey just after Passover week."

Leah smiled as she looked down at the vegetables she was cutting for the soup pot.

"And how was your day, wife?" asked Jacob.

Leah was in thought and answered, "It has been wonderful, Jacob. Jacob, we are blessed. My time has not come for two months, and Mother says I must be with child. It is just as that young man said at Passover in the market. The curse has been lifted, Jacob! Jacob, did you ever hear his name?"

Jacob looked at his wife and remarked, "I believe I overheard some women and, I believe, their brother speaking of him as Jesus of Nazareth."

"What did they say, Jacob?" asked Leah.

"Just that this Jesus was from Nazareth and the son of a carpenter, but one of the sisters spoke like he was a prophet or even he might be the Messiah the scrolls speak about."

"But, Jacob, doesn't the scrolls say the Messiah will come as a great warrior? He sure didn't look or speak like a great warrior."

"I do not know, Leah. The synagogue priest and scribes say he will be a great warrior," said Jacob.

"I do not care, Jacob. Our curse has been lifted, and I bless Yahweh for that," Leah said.

PART 3

AD 18-28

CHAPTER 18

THE SOWER OF SEED AND RED DOG

FOUR YEARS HAD PASSED since the Passover where Jesus had met Lazarus, Mary, and Martha.

Jesus was now twenty-four years of age, and it was AD 18.

"Jesus!"

"Yes, Father," answered Jesus.

"I need you to hitch up the cart and take this plow I have made for Jacob at the end of town!"

"Yes, Father, I will see to it," came the reply from Jesus.

Jesus hitched their donkey to the cart, had James help him put the plow on the cart, and started off down the road to Jacob's field and house.

As he walked along leading the donkey, a red-colored dog fell in behind Jesus.

Jesus looked at the dog and asked, "What do you want, red dog?"

The dog's ears perked up, and her tail wagged, which curled up and over her back. She cocked her head to the side as if to say, "I am to walk with you, master."

Jesus laughed to himself and said, "That is all right, red dog. You can follow if you like. Just don't bother the donkey!"

As the two walked along, they came to a field that ran alongside of the road where a farmer had been sowing seed.

As Jesus looked, he saw where the sower had thrown seeds on hard ground, some on shallow ground, some on weed and nettle ground, and some on really good, fertile ground.

The birds were eating the seeds on the bare ground, and the seeds were almost gone.

It had rained that week. The seeds on the shallow ground had taken root, but the seeds in the ground with weeds and nettles had sprouted also but had to contend with the weeds that were there.

Jesus noticed that the seeds that were sown in the plowed fertile field were sprouting strong with good roots to withstand harsh conditions.

Jesus continued on his way, with the red dog following along as company.

When Jesus had delivered the plow to Jacob for his father, Jacob had a table and chair, so Jesus loaded the items to take back to his father to fix.

The next week, Joseph had fixed the table and chair for Jesus to take back to Jacob.

Jesus loaded the table and chair onto the cart and started off toward Jacob's farm.

During the week, wherever Jesus went, the red dog followed.

Jesus would wonder, *What is this animal doing?*

But Jesus knew this animal, this dog, was a friend of man and would always be such if man was a friend of them.

Men should be like animals that Yahweh had put on the earth in the beginning. They love just like Yahweh loves the children he created—unconditionally.

When the two companions came to the field that had been planted, Jesus saw the seeds on the bare ground were gone and the seeds in the shallow ground had sprung up but had withered away because they had no root system and dried out.

Then he saw the weeds choking out the seeds that had fallen there among the weeds and nettles.

But he looked at the fertile ground and saw a crop of wheat that was twenty, forty, and sixty times as much as the farmer planted.

Jesus thought, *That is how the Father's word is when it falls on men's ears. Some words are lost to the enemy. Some take root, but with no understanding, the words are wasted. Then some words get confused and entangled with other things. But the words that fall on a well-plowed and fertile mind take root and flourish* (Matthew 13:3–8).

Yes, the seeds are Yahweh's word given to men.

Jesus looked at the red dog and said, "That is right, isn't it, my friend!"

The red dog cocked her head and wagged her tail and jumped around.

They walked on to Jacob's farm on a warm spring day.

CHAPTER 19

THE CALL OF JESUS

AS JESUS AND THE red dog walked back toward Mary and Joseph's house, Jesus thought to himself and expressed his insights and views to the red dog.

"My time is growing short, red dog! And I must journey to find John so the Father's glory can come to light through the Son. I can do nothing without the Father's blessing, and his will be done. (John 5:30)

"So if the Father is willing, we will journey to Judah and the Jordan River where John is preaching. But, red dog, understand you will not be able to go with me after the Holy Spirit has come upon me, for I will be going to face temptation by the evil one," explained Jesus.

"You can journey with me to Bethany, and if Lazarus, Mary, and Martha agree, I will leave you there with them."

The red dog walked alongside Jesus, looking at the master occasionally and whimpering at Jesus's statements.

*****

"Jesus," said his mother, "did the trip to Jacob's farm go well?"

"Yes, Mother," came the reply. "The red dog and I had a pleasant trip to deliver the table and chair."

"Oh, that dog," said Mary. "She certainly is a good friend, Jesus."

After the evening meal with Joseph and Mary in the kitchen and when others went their own way, Jesus said, "Mother, Father, I must speak with you about something."

Joseph looked at Mary, and she nodded to her husband.

"What is it, Jesus?" came the reply.

"The Father has called me, and I must journey to Judah and find John so the Father's will be done!" said Jesus. "I will be gone for a while, but I will return, and you both know what my destiny is as the Messiah."

As Joseph and Mary knew what the angel had said so many years ago, they did not know the whole story that would unfold so the glory of Yahweh could be shown.

"Son," said Mary, "where will you go, and how will you live?"

"Mother, as always, Yahweh will provide for me. I will take the red dog to keep me company until I get to Bethany and Lazarus, Mary, and Martha's home."

"Son, is it time?" said Mary.

"Yes, Mother, but I will return when Yahweh wills it."

"When will you leave, Jesus?" asked Joseph.

"In the morning hour, Father, for I must reach John as soon as I am able."

*****

Through the night, Jesus prayed to the Father for a safe journey and the Father's will to be done.

In the morning before the sun rose, Mary went to Jesus's room and sat on the side of the bed.

"Jesus," she said quietly, "your father and I know one day this would come. Even with Yahweh's blessings on you, it is only natural for us, your earthly parents, to be concerned."

"Mother," Jesus said, "Father wills this, and all the events that were written in the Scriptures must manifest and come to pass so his glory can be seen. John must baptize me so Father can send the Holy Spirit to comfort and guide me on my journey."

By this time, Jesus was sitting up on his bed. Mary hugged him and told him the morning meal was ready.

When Jesus stepped out of the door, the red dog, lying by the step with her head between her front legs, jumped up and wagged her tail.

"Come on, friend," said Jesus. "We have a long journey to take."

The journey to Bethany was arduous at times for Jesus as people gathered around him to hear what this young rabbi had to speak about—the coming kingdom of God and the coming of the Messiah who was going to proclaim the righteousness of the Father.

But in due time, Jesus and the red dog arrived at Bethany and the home of Lazarus, Mary, and Martha.

Mary and Martha were elated to see Jesus, and Lazarus threw his arms around Jesus and kissed him on the cheek.

"Blessed are you, brother Lazarus. You give the Son of Man his due honor in your home."

Jesus and the red dog were made welcome by the brother and sisters, and the red dog even got to spend the night in the home.

After two days and nights, Jesus bid farewell to Lazarus, Mary, and Martha and went with their blessings on his travels. The red dog was welcomed to stay.

The red dog hugged her head as Jesus walked away, knowing that the future of the Master was in the Creator's hands.

Outside of Bethany, Jesus joined up with a small band of people from the Judah area headed for the Jordan River and John's ministry.

As they walked along, Jesus inquired into the reason the people were going to see John.

"Oh!" exclaimed one young man. "John is the reincarnated Elijah or a prophet of Yahweh."

Another said, "This prophet is baptizing repentant sinners and speaking about the coming Messiah that will come and baptize us with fire and the spirit of Yahweh!"

There was much talk about the coming of Yahweh's kingdom and overthrowing the Roman's rule in Judah and Israel.

CHAPTER 20

JESUS'S MINISTRY BEGINS

FROM HIS CHILDHOOD HOME, Nazareth, Jesus set out to begin his earthly ministry. He was baptized by John the Baptist in the Jordan River.

"Repent, for the kingdom of heaven is at hand," preached John on the banks of the Jordan.

Word had spread throughout Judah and into the Galilean area that a man many said was Elijah or the Messiah or even a prophet was baptizing for the remission of sins.

Word carried fast in the first-century Judah, especially word of a man with something new and refreshing to say.

Many came to hear John teach and preach about the Messiah who was coming to rule Israel as the king.

The teaching was different from what the temple priests and the Pharisees were teaching in Jerusalem.

For many years, so-called messiahs had risen up with followers, only to be disbanded and scattered after the "messiahs" were arrested and executed for sedition or rebellion against the temple priests and Roman authority in Jerusalem.

"This will not continue," vowed the Sanhedrin council. "We will investigate this preacher in the desert who wears animal skins for clothes and eats locust and honey like a wild man."

*****

Events surrounding Jesus's baptism revealed the intensive religious excitement and social ferment of the early days of John the Baptist's ministry. Herod had been rapacious and extravagant: Roman military occupation was harsh in the Judahian area without hesitation of the guards toward the Jewish faction.

Some agitation to their harshness centered around the change in governors from Gratus to Pilate in AD 26.

Most people hoped for a religious solution to their situation, and when they heard of a new prophet, they flocked out to the desert along the banks of the Jordan River to see and hear John preach.

The religious sect at that time, the Essenes from the Qumran area of the Dead Sea, professed similar doctrines of repentance and baptism.

*****

Jesus was baptized at Bethany on the east side of the Jordan River (John 1:28).

But also John was baptizing at the Aenon, near the town of Salim. (John 3:23)

"Repent, for the kingdom of heaven is near. I am crying in the wilderness, saying, 'Repentance of sins for your transgressions.'"

The Jews at the temple of Jerusalem had sent priests and Levites to ask John, "Who are you?"

John confessed, "I am not the Christ, the Anointed One!" (John 1:19).

Then the Priests asked him, "What then? Are you Elijah?"

He said, "I am not!"

"Are you a prophet?" they inquired.

John answered, "No!"

Then they said to John, "Who are you that we may give an answer to those who sent us."

John looked at them and said, "I am the voice of the one crying in the wilderness. Make straight the way of the Lord, as it is written in scroll of Prophet Isaiah" (John 1:23).

The priests who had been sent to confront John were the Pharisees.

They asked John, "Why baptize you then if you are not the Christ, the Anointed One, Elijah, or a prophet?"

John answered them, saying, "I baptize with water. There comes one among you whom you will not know. He who comes after me is preferred over me, whose sandals I am not worthy to unloose!

"One mightier than me will baptize you with the Holy Ghost and with fire" (John 1:20–26).

*****

Two days later, in Bethany on the east side of the Jordan River, John was standing in the water preaching the kingdom and repentance of sins when he looked up toward the multitude of people on the bank and saw Jesus walking toward him.

"Behold!" shouted John. "The Lamb of Yahweh, who takes away the sins of the world" (John 1:29).

Jesus walked in between the mass of people standing on the bank and waded into the river's current to where John stood.

"This is the one I have preached about," said John.

John was gazing at Jesus, who approached John and said, "John, I have come to be baptized by you as my time has come!"

But John tried to prevent Jesus from being baptized, saying "I am the one that needs to be baptized by you, and you are coming to me?" (Matthew 3:15).

Jesus answered John, "Permit it to be so now, for thus it is fitting for us to fulfill all righteousness that is written" (Matthew 3:15).

John eased Jesus into the water, and as soon as he (Jesus) came up, the clouds parted. The Holy Spirit, as a dove, alighted on Jesus's shoulder.

A voice came forth from heaven, and John heard, "This is my beloved Son, in whom I am well pleased" (Matthew 3:17).

And John bore witness, saying, "I saw the spirit descending from heaven like a dove, and he remained upon him. (John 1:32).

"I did not know him but he who sent me to baptize with the Holy Spirit" (John 1:33).

"And I have seen and testify that this is the Son of Yahweh!" (John 1:34).

A little while later, John and two of his followers were standing on the bank of the Jordan when Jesus walked toward them.

"Behold, the Lamb of Yahweh," spoke John.

The two disciples, seeing the Master, left John and followed Jesus (John 1:36–37).

Jesus had returned to the wilderness after his baptism, where he had fasted for forty days and forty nights.

During the fasting and cleansing time in the desert, Christ was hungry. The devil, the evil one, came to Jesus. The tempter came to Jesus with three temptations to attack the Son of Yahweh.

In all three occasions, Satan was trying to persuade Jesus to worship the devil and his kingdom.

Jesus, using scripture, rebuked the devil and drove the evil one away from him.

By word of God, the devil will flee from you, thought Jesus.

After being tempted by the devil and the devil fled from Jesus, he was tended to by the angels. Jesus was refreshed, and the Holy Spirit led Jesus back to the banks of the Jordan to call his first disciples.

When the two disciples of John approached Jesus, he asked them, "What do you seek?"

"Rabbi!" they said. "Where are you staying?"

"Come and see," said Jesus.

One of the two who followed Jesus was Andrew, Simon Peter's brother.

Andrew brought Simon to Jesus; and as Jesus looked at Simon, he said to Simon, "You shall be called Cephas!" which is translated as "a stone."

The next day, Jesus wanted to go to Galilee; and when he found Phillip, he said, "Follow me."

Phillip was from Bethsaida, the city of Andrew and Simon Peter.

Phillip found Nathanael and said to him, "We have found him. We have him whom Moses spoke about in the law and also the prophets wrote, Jesus of Nazareth, the son of Joseph the carpenter."

Nathanael scoffed at Phillip and said, "Can anything good come out of Nazareth?"

"Come and see," said Philip.

As Phillip and Nathanael approached Jesus and the others he had called to his discipleship, Jesus said, "Behold, an Israelite indeed, in whom there is no deceit."

Nathanael was perplexed and said, "How do you know me?"

Jesus smiled and gave a little laugh. "Before Phillip called you, when you were under the fig tree, I saw you!"

Nathanael fell to his knees with his mouth agape and said, "You are the Son of God, the king of Israel."

"Do you believe because I said, 'I saw you under the fig tree'? You will see greater things than these!" exclaimed Jesus. Then Jesus went on, "Most assuredly, I say to you. Hereafter you shall see heaven open and the angels of God ascending and descending upon the Son of Man!" (John 1:46–45).

CHAPTER 21

MAGDALA

THE YEAR WAS AD 23. Jesus and John were both twenty-nine years of age.

John had been preaching in the area around the Jordan as Yahweh had willed, prior to being thrown in prison.

Jesus was preaching in and around Galilee as "his time had not yet come," according to the will of Yahweh.

When the group of disciples of Jesus approached Magdala, Jesus fretted about the dark cloud that hung over the fishing and boat-building community.

As they walked along, Jesus was thinking to himself and said, "Truly I tell you. There are dark visions I see here. We must truly be on the lookout for the evil one's followers, for they are all around us in this town."

As the group came to the marketplace, there was a large group of people pushing and shoving each other, trying to get to the front of the crowd.

Jesus and his group moved to one side of the crowd so they could see what was happening there.

Jesus saw a young woman, about the age of twenty-three or twenty-four, standing in the middle of the crowd with three other men beside her shouting and saying, "If you desire her to tell you your fortune, the price is one denarius."

"One day's wages to learn about the rest of your life," barked the other man.

The young woman was foaming at the mouth, eyes rolling back into her eye sockets and speaking in an unknown tongue.

She abruptly stopped dancing around and stared at Jesus, her head switching from side to side.

She then continued to move around in a circle within the crowd.

Jesus shouted, "Stop, evil spirits! Do not torment her any longer! Come out of her and leave her be," commanded Jesus.

The crowd did not hear the voice that emanated from the young woman, but Jesus heard them.

"Leave me be, Jesus, Son of the Most High. We have nothing to do with you, and she is ours."

"In the name of El Shaddai, Almighty Yahweh, I command you seven demons to come out of her and be gone!"

At that moment, the young woman fell to the ground and twitched and shook and then lay still.

"What have you done?" bellowed one of the men. "She was making money for us, and you have ruined all that. What shall wo do now?"

Jesus looked at the three men and said, "Be off and leave her alone!"

One of Jesus's disciples bent down over the young woman, helping her stand.

Jesus had walked over to where she stood and inquired, "Mary, are you all right?"

Mary of Magdala looked at Jesus and asked, "Rabbi, how did you know my name?"

Jesus answered, "Mary, I have always known you from the time your mother and father were thinking of conceiving you until now. Go home and be assured. The evil one will not bother you anymore."

Mary brushed herself off, straightened her dress and cloak, and ventured home.

When she turned to walk away, Jesus said to her, "Mary, do as Yahweh wills for you and do not question the commands."

Mary turned and looked at the group of young and old men and asked, "How will I know Yahweh's commands?"

Jesus said, "Mary, you will know, and Yahweh will guide you.

*****

Mary was wondering all the way home what all this meant to her.

She knew for certain something had come over her spirit.

"Mother, Father!" shouted Mary as she entered her father's house. "The most wonderful thing has happened to me in the marketplace. The demons that possessed me for oh so many months were thrown out by a rabbi just today. He even knew my name and said he had known me from before you and mother conceived me in mother's womb."

Mary's mother and father looked at Mary and inquired, "How can this be, daughter?"

"I do not know, Mother. All I know is the rabbi—his name is Jesus—told me to let Yahweh guide me and I would know when Yahweh calls me."

Through the night, Mary thought about all the events of the previous day and how her spirits had soared as she walked back home.

As Mary slept, a vision came to her in the form of a dream—children playing, sitting, and listening to Jesus talking.

Mary slept soundly the rest of the night.

The next morning, she went to her mother and father and told them, "Mother, Father, I had a dream last night of the rabbi telling the children to come to him and believe on the Father in heaven's word. Father, I believe I am to follow this rabbi and be of help to his ministry as best as I can.

"Father, you know that brother is destined to inherit the ship-building company you built, and I have no other responsibilities here. I ask your permission to follow this rabbi, for I feel he may be the Messiah the scrolls speak of told by the great prophets."

Mary's mother and father had talked about the events in Mary's life and agreed, if Yahweh did in fact call Mary to help this young rabbi's ministry, she should do as Yahweh wills.

"So be it, daughter," her father said. "Take what you need in the cart. You can take the young donkey in the corral. I will send a messenger to you each month with an allowance to see you through until the next month. Go in peace, Mary, and Yahweh's blessings be with you until you return to us."

Mary got busy and packed all she thought she would need on the trail and extra for the group of men who followed Jesus.

She set off to find the group of men with Jesus; and thankfully she found them a few hundred yards out of town, not having broke camp to leave for the next town, which was Nazareth, Jesus's home.

Jesus turned and saw Mary Magdalene leading the colt donkey and cart.

"Welcome, Mary. Join us please," said Jesus.

Through his greetings, he heard some of the followers mumbling some discontent.

"We are pleased to have you join us on our journeys. May Yahweh bless you as you travel with us."

Nothing else was said among the disciples of Jesus as he turned and started on his way.

CHAPTER 22

TWO HOUSES AND CANA

A S TIME PROGRESSED IN early Judah, Jesus's teaching had spread to the nearby villages, where a few men other than the four disciples were communing with him.

Jesus and a few of the followers were eating the noon meal under some trees outside of Nazareth.

"And just what is the kingdom of Yahweh you speak of, Jesus?"

"I tell you the truth, Phillip," said Jesus. "The man that hears the word of the Father and believes it is like one who builds his house on solid ground (Matthew 7:24–27).

"When trials and tribulations come in the form of storms and floods, his house will stand against all disasters. But the man who hears the word and does not believe it is like a man who builds his house on shifting sands. When trials and tribulations come his way, the foundation is eroded, and this washes away all his understanding.

"Brothers, verily, verily I say to you. You must believe every word of Yahweh and the one he sent to carry out his will. There is no other way than to believe the very word of God."

Mary was sitting at Jesus's feet, looking at the Master.

"Who, Jesus, is the one you keep talking and telling us about? To do the Father's will?"

Jesus looked at the young man listening to him and said, "His time has not come for the glory of the Father to be revealed, but soon his glory will be seen."

When the young man following Jesus approached Joseph and Mary's house, Mary stepped out into the yard and said to Jesus, "We have been invited to one of your cousin's wedding in Cana of Galilee. Would you and your friends like to attend? They are welcomed also."

The young disciples at the time looked at Jesus and said, "Yes, we would be pleased to attend."

*****

The next morning, the young disciples met Jesus and Mary at the house of Joseph.

The cart was hitched to the donkey and filled with wedding gifts while Mary of Magdala followed with her own donkey and cart.

As they started off, one young man took the rope lead from Mary's hand and told her he would be glad to lead the donkey for Jesus's mother.

Mary thanked him and slipped back a bit behind Jesus who was walking with the five or six young men.

Many things were discussed on their way to Cana.

Jesus talked about the kingdom of Yahweh being likened to a merchant who discovered a great treasure in a field he did not own.

"The merchant went back and sold all his possessions so he could buy the field. (Matthew 13:44)

"That is like the treasure of the kingdom of Heaven," said Jesus. "To get the treasure, we should be willing to give up all we have to be allowed to enter."

The young men, even though they had been with Jesus for weeks, said among themselves, "We are astonished at his teachings. He speaks as one with great authority."

When they reached the outskirts of Cana, Jesus said to all who heard, "Let us go and enjoy the wedding and festivities that are offered to us."

With that, the group of followers and Jesus followed Mary to the cousin's house.

*****

The next day, the wedding took place, and everyone celebrated two hands becoming one.

Jesus spoke to the others when the service was over, "This is the way the Father intended, man and woman to dwell together, two people joining together to form one person. Man and woman, as it was in the garden, are meant to celebrate life and the forming of life and dwell in harmony together.

"For the Father said, 'Go forth and populate the earth'" (Genesis 1:28).

The celebration was going well, with all having a wonderful time.

Jesus had noticed the headwaiter saying something to his mother, Mary.

Mary approached Jesus and told him, "They have run out of wine to serve the guests."

Jesus said to her, "Woman, what does that concern have to do with me? My hour has not yet come!" (John 2:4).

Mary did not take this statement of Jesus to be a rebuff but told the servants, "Whatever he says to you, do it!" (John 2:7).

There were six waterpots made of stone, according to the purification of Jews, containing twenty or thirty gallons of water apiece.

Jesus told the servants to fill the pots with water. They filled the pots to the brim.

Jesus told one of the servants to take some of the liquid to the master of the feast.

When the servant did as Jesus requested, the master tasted the liquid that had been turned to wine and said, "Take this to the bridegroom to taste also." The master of the feast said to the bridegroom, "Every man at the beginning sets out the good wine until all are drunk, then he sets out the inferior wine."

"But, sir, you have kept the good wine for last" (John 2:10).

This was the beginning of Jesus's manifestation of Yahweh's glory.

His disciples saw and believed him.

CHAPTER 23

THE DECISION

WHEN MARY RETURNED TO Nazareth and their home, she found Joseph sitting at the table he had built.

Joseph had a scroll in his hand, lying on the tabletop and studying the writing.

"What is it, husband?" asked Mary.

Joseph looked at her and asked her to sit down.

Mary sat down and folded her hands on top of the table.

"What is it, husband?" she inquired.

Joseph took his eyes off of the scroll and turned the scroll around for Mary to be able to read.

Then he straightened up and looked at his wife, only to say, "Mary, a while back, remember I told you that our friend in Jerusalem was wanting us to move there to help him in his carpenter shop?"

Mary shook her head and said, "Of course, I remember!"

"In this scroll he wrote to me, his business is growing more than he is able to by himself. He has no one to help him, so he has offered me a position in his employment with a very good wage, more than I am making now. It will mean moving and taking the children with us, those who desire to go."

Mary thought for a second and said, "As you wish, husband." Then Mary interjected, "Joseph, Jesus has manifested the glory that is Yahweh at Cana, and I feel he will be leaving us soon. James and the other children will surely go with us as there is no growth here in Nazareth."

*****

When the other children gathered around the evening meal table, Mary looked at the boys. She stopped and thought these were men and young men seated at the table. She glanced over at where Simone would have been sitting, but she thought it had been a year since Simone was wed and moved to Jerusalem with her husband.

"Children"—and she used the term loosely, for these men were still her children—"your father has some news to share with you."

Joseph had passed the bread after breaking it and blessing the meal. "We will be moving to Jerusalem after the next Sabbath. The work in Nazareth has grown slow, and it is hard to furnish all our needs. I have been offered employment there with a friend of ours.

"James, Jesus, you two brothers are old enough to decide your own path to take, and Mary and I will not stand in your way."

Jesus knew the day was coming, so he waited for James to speak first.

James looked at his father and mother and said, "Father, if Yahweh wills it, I will go with you and Mother, Joses, and Judas." Judas would later change his name to Jude to keep from being identified as Judas Iscariot. "I will find work in Jerusalem and help you move," said James.

The two younger brothers sat there and listened to their parents talk and what was in store for them.

Finally Jesus spoke. Mary and Joseph had been waiting for him to speak.

"Mother, Father, you know as well as I know my time draws near. I know that John preaches in the area around the Jordan River and will pave the way for the Messiah, which Isaiah foretold by the spirit of Yahweh.

"A voice of one crying in the desert, 'Prepare the way of the Lord, make straight in the wilderness a highway for Yahweh!' (Matthew 3:3)

"I must be after my Father's business until that time comes."

Mary thought back to that day in the synagogue in Jerusalem when Jesus was twelve years old. That was when Jesus had first used these words.

James looked at Jesus and said, "This is your father's business, Jesus!"

James put down his napkin without folding it (as it was the Jewish custom to fold the napkin after one was finished eating) and left the table.

Mary started to go after James, but Jesus said, "Let me talk to James, Mother. He will understand!"

Jesus followed James into the yard and stood behind him.

"James," said Jesus, "listen to me. There are things that Yahweh wills that you as a human cannot understand. There will come a time in the near future that your eyes will be opened to the glory of Yahweh, and you will play a part larger than you can imagine!

"James, even though it might be hard for you to see at present, you will be a part of Yahweh's glory. Take care of Mother and Father and see to their needs as Yahweh directs you. Love me as I have always loved you, brother."

*****

James walked back into the house, dumbfounded and puzzled.

Mary asked, "James, are you all right?"

James sat down to finish his meal and said to Mary, "Mother, I am confused. What does Jesus mean I am to play a part in Yahweh's glory?"

Mary smiled and went over to James and said softly, "James, we all wonder at Yahweh's glory and how we are to play a part. For it says in Isaiah that Yahweh's ways are not our ways and his thoughts are not our thoughts (Isaiah 55:8).

"We have to wait and see as his will is revealed to us." Mary hugged her son and kissed him on his cheek.

CHAPTER 24

FOXES HAVE HOLES

JESUS HELPED JAMES AND Joseph load the wagon with the belongings of the family and helped Mary up into the seat of the cart.

As he was doing so, Mary turned to Jesus and said, "So your father and I knew this day was coming, but it still isn't easy for us to understand why Yahweh has willed this to happen."

Jesus looked at his mother and said, "Mother, this day has been ordained since Adam and Eve, the first man and woman, disobeyed the Father. These things must happen before mankind can find righteousness in the Father's eyes."

Tears welled up in Mary's eyes. She leaned down and kissed Jesus on the cheek. "May Yahweh take care of you, Jesus, and may his blessings be with you."

Joseph and James said goodbye, along with Joses and Judas (later to be named Jude).

As they walked away, Jesus pulled the hood of his cloak up over his head to ward off the cold of the morning dew.

As he turned around, there stood three of his followers who had been with them since the start in Cana and some before.

The red dog barked at them, but Jesus didn't reprimand the dog.

"Where will you go, Rabbi?" asked the older of the three.

Jesus looked at him and said, "Foxes have holes, and birds of the sky have nests, but the Son of Man has nowhere to lay his head (Matthew 8:20).

"We go where Yahweh leads us, and if the town we are in does not accept or welcome us, we will shake the dust off of our sandals and continue our journey.

"For the prophet is not welcomed in his own hometown" (Luke 4:24).

One of the young men said, "Rabbi, first I must go and bury my father!"

Jesus looked at the young man with concern and said, "Follow me and let the dead bury the dead."

With this, the other followers went with Jesus toward the Galilean area.

CHAPTER 25

THE BEGINNING OF THE BEGINNING

AD 24 FOUND JESUS and his followers leaving Nazareth where they had stayed for a short time.

Jesus had not performed any signs or miracles in his hometown as he had not found any faith or belief there.

"Are you not Joseph and Mary's son?" Are you not the carpenter's son?" asked the people of Nazareth.

Jesus and his followers shook the dust off of their sandals and went on to Capernaum.

When they reached Peter's house, there were mourners in the yard and house.

Peter ran ahead of the group and came out to tell Jesus Peter's mother-in-law was sick with a fever.

Jesus asked Peter, "Where is she, brother?"

Peter, crying, indicated she was on a bed in the house.

Jesus entered the house and bent over Peter's mother-in-law and rebuked the fever, and it left her (Matthew 8:14).

She got up at once and began to wait on the followers.

*****

When their ministry had completed its work in Capernaum, they headed south toward the Jordan River.

As they walked along the banks of the Sea of Galilee, Jesus came upon some fishermen tending their nets.

Jesus immediately saw James and John, sons of Zebedee, whom he had seen with John his cousin.

"Follow me," announced Jesus. "I will make you fishers of men" (Mark 1:17).

The two brothers dropped their nets, told their father they were to follow this rabbi, and went with him.

For they had remembered the same voice and exclamation given to them so many years before.

Both James and John, sons of Zebedee, told their father, "Father, we must follow Rabbi. He speaks the truth."

Many years later, John would become the apostle the Scriptures speak about, "the one whom the Messiah loved."

*****

The troop of followers and the Messiah traveled throughout Judah and Galilee areas, going where the Spirit led them.

They spent time in Bethany with Lazarus, Mary, and Martha, who were more than willing to entertain the troop of followers and Jesus.

Back up through Judah and into the Galilean area by the Sea of Galilee and cape, John had established his ministry in and around the Jordan River.

CHAPTER 26

RESURRECTION OF LAZARUS

"**M**ARY, MARTHA, PLEASE COME quick!" shouted Lazarus from his bed in the house. "I cannot eat or drink any nourishment! I do not know what is wrong with me."

Mary and Martha hurried to their brother's side to see what might be the problem with Lazarus.

"Mary," Martha said, "our brother is burning up with fever and sweats terribly. What can be the problem?"

Bethany, on the west side of the Jordan River, was only two miles from Jerusalem, on the downward slope toward the Salt Sea (Dead Sea).

"What should we do?" asked Mary. "We keep him bathed and cool and see if the fever breaks."

As the day progressed, Lazarus continued to get worse and became delirious with the fever.

Mary had become frantic with worry and told her sister, "We must send for the Messiah to come. If he is here, our brother will be healed."

Mary and Martha searched Bethany for a messenger to send to find Jesus on the other side of the Jordan River.

"Please, good man," Martha said, "tell the rabbi that Lazarus, the one whom he loves, is very sick!"

With instructions to search the area around Bethabara, the Bethany on the eastern side of the Jordan, the young messenger started on his way.

After two days, the messenger said, "I have been sent by the sisters of Lazarus, the one whom you love, to tell you he is very sick!"

When Jesus heard the news, he said, "This sickness is not unto death but the glory of the Father, that the Son of Man can be glorified through it" (John 11:4).

So when he heard that Lazarus was sick, he and his followers stayed two more days where they were.

As dawn broke on the third day after receiving the message, Jesus said to his followers, "Let us go to Judah again."

The disciples were worried and said to him, "Rabbi, lately the Jews sought to stone you, and you are going there again?" (John 11:8).

"Our friend Lazarus sleeps, but I go that I may wake him," came the reply from Jesus.

"Lord, if he sleeps, he will get well!" said the disciples.

Jesus thought to himself, *They think Lazarus is only asleep, so I must tell them.*

"Lazarus is dead," came his reply. "I am glad that, for your sake, I was not there, that you may believe" (John 11:15).

Thomas, the disciple who was known as Didymus (the twin) and doubter, said to the other disciples, "Let us go, that we may die with him!" (John 11:16).

When Jesus came to Bethany, he found out Lazarus had been dead and in the tomb for four days.

Many Jews had gathered, with the women around Mary and Martha to comfort them concerning their brother.

When Martha heard Jesus was coming, she ran and met him, but Mary had stayed at the house (John 11:20).

"Lord!" exclaimed Martha. "If you had been here, my brother would not have died (John 11:21).

"But with you now, I know that, whatever you ask of Yahweh, Yahweh will give it to you!"

Jesus asked Martha, "Do you believe Lazarus will rise again?"

Martha looked at Jesus and said, "Yes, I know he will rise at the resurrection on the last day."

Jesus said, "Martha, I am the resurrection and the life. He who believes in me, though he may die, shall rise again and live (John 11:25).

"And whoever lives and believes in me shall never die. Do you believe this?"

"Yes, Lord," came Martha's reply. "I believe that you are the Christ, the Son of God, who is to come into the world" (John 11:27).

Jesus had Mary, who had come to him when he had sent Martha back to the house to get her, to show him the tomb Lazarus was laid in.

"Lord, come and see," said Mary.

As Jesus looked upon the tomb sealed off with a large stone, he wept (John 11:35).

"Take away the stone," commanded Jesus.

Mary interjected her thoughts to the Messiah, "Lord, by this time, there is a stench for he has been dead for four days."

"Mary, did I not tell you that, if you would only believe, you would see the glory of Yahweh?" (John 11:40).

With the tombstone rolled away, Jesus lifted his eyes up toward heaven and said, "Father, I thank you that you have heard me (John 11:41).

"And I know that you always hear me, but because of these people who are standing by, I said this, that they may believe that you sent me!" (John 11:42).

When Jesus had said these things, he cried out with a loud voice, "Lazarus, come forth" (John 11:43).

Lazarus, who had closed his eyes four days earlier, opened his eyes, saw the light coming from the tomb entrance, and thought, *What am I doing here in these burial clothes?*

It was like no more than a twinkling of an eye that he had been sick on his bed in the house.

He heard the Master's voice calling his name. He got up on his feet and walked to the tomb entrance.

When he appeared at the tomb's entrance, Jesus said, "Loose him and let him go."

Many people who had come to comfort Mary and Martha believed in Jesus.

But there were the disbelievers and unbelievers among the people there that day.

Some of the unbelievers went to the Pharisees and priests of the Sanhedrin to tell of the events in Bethany that day.

Upon news of the resurrection of Lazarus, the Pharisees called a council meeting.

"What shall we do? For this man works many signs. If we do not stop him, he will continue, and everyone will believe him."

"If we do not stop him, he will continue. Then the Romans will come and take away both our places in the temple and our nation."

Caiaphas, the high priest that year, said to them, "You know nothing at all.

"Nor do you consider that it is expedient for us that one man should die for the people and not that a nation should perish" (John 11:50).

Even though Caiaphas did not say these things with his own authority, being high priest that year, he prophesized that Jesus would die for the nation.

From that day on, the Sanhedrin plotted to put Jesus, the Messiah, to death.

Word got back to Jesus and the disciples, so they did not walk openly among the Jews. He took the disciples, left Bethany, ventured into the wilderness to a city called Ephraim, and remained there.

CHAPTER 27

THE ANOINTING AND
SATAN'S WORK

A S THE NEWS SPREAD of Jesus's great sign in Bethany, the Pharisees had given a command that, if anyone knew where Jesus was, they should report it so the Sanhedrin might seize him.

By now, the disciples had grown to twelve apostles and many followers.

Among them was Judas Iscariot, the one who would betray the Christ.

Mary Magdalene was also among the group of followers.

Six days before the Passover, Jesus had come to Bethany where Lazarus was, who had been raised from the dead (John 12:1).

The sisters, Mary and Martha, had made him a supper; and Martha served. Lazarus sat at the table with Jesus.

As Jesus taught at the table, with all listening, Mary took a pound of expensive spikenard, anointed Jesus's feet, and wiped his feet with her hair (John 12:3).

The aroma filled the house with the fragrance of the oil; but there was one of Jesus's followers, Judas Iscariot, Simon's son, who said, "Why was this fragrant oil not sold for three hundred denarii and given to the poor?" (John 12:5).

This was only a ruse of Judas as he was the holder of the group's purse and all moneys they had.

In his heart, which Jesus knew, grew a cold, hard stone that only wanted to get his hands on the money for himself.

"Let her alone," Jesus said. "She has kept this for the day of my burial (John 12:7).

"For the poor you will always have, but for me, you do not always have" (John 12:8).

Many of the Jews in the Judah area came not just for Jesus's sake but also because of Lazarus's, whom Jesus had raised from the dead.

During this time, the priests and Pharisees had plotted to kill Lazarus also. Because of him, many Jews went away and believed in Jesus.

As Jesus spoke, he said to all listening, but looked at Judas, "Truly I tell you. You cannot serve two masters. No servant can serve two masters, for either he will hate one and love the other, or else he will love and be loyal to the one and despise the other. You cannot serve God and mammon" (Luke 16:13).

After this, Judas Iscariot went to the temple priests in Jerusalem and inquired of them, "What will you give me if I deliver him"—Jesus—"to you?" (Matthew 26:14–15).

The temple priests counted out thirty pieces of silver and gave it to Judas. The devil had done its work.

CHAPTER 28

THE GLORIOUS ENTRY
(PALM SUNDAY)

THREE DAYS LATER, THE first day of the week and the start of Passover week, Jesus gathered his flock together and told them, "It is time for us to journey to Jerusalem for the Passover."

Jesus called John, the brother of James, and Andrew, the brother of Peter, to go to the city; and they would find a post in front of a potter's shop where a colt donkey was tied up.

"The colt had never been ridden. Untie it and bring it back to where I would be. If the owner inquires of your need of the colt, tell him, 'The Master needs the use of it.'"

The two set off toward Jerusalem before the others got started on their way.

When John and Andrew entered the city, the mass of people had started gathering, for the news that the Messiah was to be in the city had spread throughout Judah.

John and Andrew walked the streets of the lower city looking for a colt tied to a hitching post.

Just then, Andrew called out, "There!" and pointed toward a she-donkey and her colt tied to a post in front of a pottery shop.

Jacob, the shop's owner, was spinning a lump of clay on his potter's wheel when John and Andrew came through the front door.

"Yes, kind sirs," said Jacob, "what may I do for you?"

Andrew was the first to speak. "Sir, Is that your she-donkey and colt tied out front?"

"Yes," answered Jacob.

John said, "May we use the colt?"

Jacob looked at the two disciples and asked, "What, may I ask, are you going to do with the colt?"

Andrew told Jacob, "The Master has need of the colt since it has not been ridden."

Jacob thought for a moment, then said, "Is this Master Jesus of Nazareth?"

"Yes, he is."

"Then by all means, the colt is yours for the Messiah to use. We, my wife and I, have been blessed some years ago, and now we thank Yahweh for the Messiah."

Jacob rose up from the potter's wheel, bowed to John and Andrew, and bid them farewell.

On their way back out of town, John and Andrew saw visitors laying down palm branches in the street of Jerusalem.

The temple priests were milling around talking to the visitors and watching the activities of all in the streets and shops.

As John and Andrew approached Jesus and the others, they were taking their cloaks off.

When they came to where Jesus was standing, the colt was standing tall and sided up to Jesus.

John told Jesus, "The colt was tied up outside of a potter's shop."

"Yes, John," said Jesus, "that was Jacob's shop, whom I met in the marketplace some time ago."

Thomas spread his cloak on the donkey colt and helped Jesus up onto the back of the colt.

Jesus looked down at the red dog, who was sitting on her hunches looking at the Master.

"Yes, red dog," said Jesus, "you may lead the way into the city for us."

The red dog jumped up and ran around in a circle, making sure she did not frighten the colt.

As the group started entering the outskirts of Jerusalem, the people started gathering and singing psalms.

The people had grown to a point that there were shoving and pushing among themselves, lining the streets on the outside of the city walls.

As the colt carrying Jesus, led by the red dog, entered through the Golden Gate of the city, a mighty roar went up.

The people started singing: "Hosanna, hosanna to the son of David. Blessed is his name, who comes in the name of the Lord" (Matthew 14:3).

Some of the Pharisees called to Jesus from the crowd lining the streets, "Teacher, rebuke your disciples!"

But Jesus answered them, "I tell you the truth that, if these should be silent, the very stones would immediately cry out" (Luke 19:39–40).

This was the first day of the last week of Jesus's earthly life.

But we know that this week was only the beginning of the real story of our Lord and Savior, Christ Jesus. He came to seek the lost, then paid for their sins on the cross!

The End

AFTERWORD

In the beginning was the Word, and the Word was with God, and the Word was God.

He was in the beginning with God, and all things were made through Him, and without Him nothing was made that was made.

In Him was life, and life was the light of all men.

And the light shines in the darkness and the darkness did not comprehend it. (John 1:1–5)

There was a man sent from God whose name was John. This man came for a witness, to bear witness of the Light, that all through him might believe. (John 1:6–7)

THROUGH THIS NARRATIVE, I have tried to put some humanity in the central characters of Christ Jesus and John the Baptist.

By no means have I tried to infringe on the divinity of Christ but to try and show the humanity of the being of God manifested in his Son—Jesus of Nazareth, a human baby and born of a virgin—and his cousin John.

Sometimes events may be out of order and context of the Scriptures, but by no means do I try to imply that this work is authentic in nature.

This narrative was written to answer some of the questions that were not approached or alluded to in the writing of the Holy Scriptures.

I sincerely hope, to my readers, this was as much fun to read as it was to write.

Thank you for taking your time to read this work.

Thank you.

ABOUT THE AUTHOR

WALTER, IN HIS SEVENTIES, lives in Mobile, Alabama, with his wife and two sons.

Having played golf in college, his golf skills have stayed with him throughout his life.

Now retired, Walter plays golf two days a week in a seniors league.

Walter got the inspiration to write *The Hidden Years* while incarcerated, which gave him time to study the Gospel and formulate a theme around the life of and the people associated with Christ.

CPSIA information can be obtained
at www.ICGtesting.com
Printed in the USA
LVHW020420170322
713568LV00007B/653